*Cowboy at Heart*

## SHIPMENT ONE

## SHIPMENT THREE

## SHIPMENT FOUR

## SHIPMENT FIVE

*Belonging to Bandera* by Tina Leonard
*Court Me, Cowboy* by Barbara White Daille
*His Best Friend's Bride* by Jodi O'Donnell
*The Cowboy's Return* by Linda Warren
*Baby Be Mine* by Victoria Pade
*The Cattle Baron* by Margaret Way

## SHIPMENT SIX

*Crockett's Seduction* by Tina Leonard
*Coming Home to the Cattleman* by Judy Christenberry
*Almost Perfect* by Judy Duarte
*Cowboy Dad* by Cathy McDavid
*Real Cowboys* by Roz Denny Fox
*The Rancher Wore Suits* by Rita Herron
*Falling for the Texas Tycoon* by Karen Rose Smith

## SHIPMENT SEVEN

*Last's Temptation* by Tina Leonard
*Daddy by Choice* by Marin Thomas
*The Cowboy, the Baby and the Bride-to-Be* by Cara Colter
*Luke's Proposal* by Lois Faye Dyer
*The Truth About Cowboys* by Margot Early
*The Other Side of Paradise* by Laurie Paige

## SHIPMENT EIGHT

*Mason's Marriage* by Tina Leonard
*Bride at Briar's Ridge* by Margaret Way
*Texas Bluff* by Linda Warren
*Cupid and the Cowboy* by Carol Finch
*The Horseman's Son* by Delores Fossen
*Cattleman's Bride-to-Be* by Lois Faye Dyer

**The rugged, masculine and independent men
of America's West know the value of hard work,
honor and family. They may be ranchers, tycoons
or the guy next door, but they are all cowboys at heart.
Don't miss any of the books in this collection!**

Cowboy at Heart

# THE RANCHER WORE SUITS
# RITA HERRON

**H HARLEQUIN® COWBOY AT HEART**

ISBN-13: 978-0-373-82638-4

THE RANCHER WORE SUITS

Copyright © 2002 by Rita B. Herron

This edition published by arrangement with Harlequin Books S.A.

For questions and comments about the quality of this book, please contact us at CustomerService@Harlequin.com.

Printed in U.S.A.

www.Harlequin.com

## RITA HERRON

Award-winning author Rita Herron wrote her first book when she was twelve, but didn't think real people grew up to be writers. Now she writes so she doesn't have to get a real job. A former kindergarten teacher and workshop leader, she traded storytelling to kids for writing romance, and now she writes romantic comedies and romantic suspense. She lives in Georgia with her own romance hero and three kids. She loves to hear from readers, so please write her at P.O. Box 921225, Norcross, GA 30092-1225, or visit her website, www.ritaherron.com.

# Prologue

*O'Hare Airport*

What else could go wrong?

As if his godawful trip to Chicago hadn't been bad enough, Ty Cooper glanced at the overhead screen and noticed his flight back to Montana had been delayed. Two hours.

More time to think about the deal that had slipped through his fingers this week.

He might as well settle in, have a drink and try to come up with some ideas to expand his cattle business. The investor he'd met with in Chicago had promised big things for the Coopers' shrinking cattle market, but all that fancy talk across conference tables hadn't seemed practical to Ty. Ty and the five generations of Coopers who'd run the Circle C were men who lived off the land, not men who wore suits, talked stock options and thought about marketing strategies. His grandparents had done without the niceties in life, and Ty wanted to give them all the luxuries they had never had. After all, he owed them so much....

A pretty little waitress smiled at him, and he tipped his Stetson, then laid it on his knee as she approached. He might be in a foul mood but Ty Cooper's grandma had raised him right—a man always behaved like a gentleman in the presence of a lady.

"Can I get you a drink, sir?"

"A beer'll be fine, sugar. Whatever you've got on tap." He winked. "I'm not picky."

She gave him that funny grin, the same one everyone in Chicago had given him for the past week every time he'd spoken. They probably didn't see too many real-life cowboys in the Windy City. A few seconds later, the waitress left him a full cold mug and he sipped the beer while he studied the report from the investor.

There was no way he could make this deal work, he realized seconds into the reading. He had to face the grim truth; there would be no upgrading at the Circle C this year. Disappointment ballooned in his chest. He'd wanted to hire an extra hand so his grandfather wouldn't have to work so hard. Pa Cooper was getting on in years. Ty worried he'd wear himself out. He also wanted his grandfather and grandmother to be able to spend more time together, take a trip, enjoy the good life in their golden years. Do things they had never done.

Frustrated, he glanced up, wishing he had a cigarette, but he'd given them up years ago, so he searched for the waitress's smile again, the only bright spot in a dismal day. Instead, his gaze landed on a man across the room and he froze, his mug lifted halfway to his mouth.

The man looked to be his height and wore one of those expensive dark suits with a red power tie. The hair on the back of Ty's neck stood on end. Something about the stranger seemed familiar.

Eerily familiar.

Then the man turned and looked straight at Ty. Shock rode through Ty's system, as it obviously did the other man. Ty could have been looking in a mirror. What the...? The man looked exactly like *him*. Same thick dark hair, only cropped a little shorter than Ty's. Same dark eyes...same square jaw... same...everything.

The man suddenly pushed to his feet, his mouth gaping open momentarily before he snapped it closed. He strode toward Ty, his back ramrod straight. He stopped in front of Ty's table, shifted his drink to his left hand and extended his right.

"Dex Montgomery."

His voice even sounded like Ty's, although he had a slight Southern intonation. Not much, though. Judging from the man's expensive clothes, he came from too much money and education to allow himself a true Southern accent.

Ty closed his work-roughened hand over the man's smooth one. "Ty Cooper."

The contact was brief, but something passed between them—energy that felt strange yet oddly familiar. As if they had some connection.

Ridiculous.

"Maybe you'd better sit down," Ty said, grappling for an explanation.

The stranger tugged at his tie as if it was choking him and sat. "This isn't possible. I mean..." He shook his head again. "I'm a doctor and even I'm at a loss for an explanation."

Ty scrubbed his hand over his chin. He had no idea what to say, either. "You're right, partner. It's damned weird looking at your reflection in another man's face. Maybe we're related somehow?" A nervous laugh escaped Ty. "You know, distantly. Identical cousins or something."

Dex Montgomery lifted one shoulder, then let it fall. "That's possible, I suppose." He hesitated, his eyebrows drawing together in thought. "Did you say Cooper?"

Ty nodded. "Of Rolling Bend, Montana. We have a cattle ranch called the—"

"Rolling Bend, Montana?" The man's face paled.

"Yeah?" Ty's stomach knotted. "You know the place?"

Dex's gaze settled fully onto Ty. "My mother's name was Tara Cooper. She was born in Rolling Bend."

It couldn't be. Ty signaled the passing waitress. "Ma'am, we're gonna need another round here."

She glanced at Dex, then started visibly when her gaze landed back on Ty. "Doubles for doubles," she said with a giggle. "Are you guys twins or something?"

Dex glared at her and she scurried away. Ty almost told him to apologize, but he was too disturbed by this man's statement. He leaned forward, unable to believe what he was about to say. "Tara Cooper was *my* mother."

A choked sound, not quite a laugh, burst from Dex. "But my mother died when I was three months old."

"My birthdate is May 21, 1970," Ty countered. "My mother died in an accident with my father when *I* was three months old."

"Oh yeah? Well, so did mine. But I don't have any siblings," Dex argued.

"Neither do I," Ty retorted. "Well, except for two adopted brothers. Actually they're my grandmother's sister's boys. She died when they were little and Gran took them in."

And Ty had had a twin who had died at birth. At least he'd been told he had. What if…what if they'd lied to him? An empty hollowness clawed at him. But why?

Dex gestured vaguely. "Maybe there were two Tara Coopers in Rolling Bend."

Ty moved his head slowly from side to side. "We're the only Cooper clan in that neck of the woods."

"I'm certain there's some reasonable explanation," Dex suggested.

Ty's heart thundered. He had a sinking feeling he knew what had happened. But he didn't like it. And judging from the shock on Dex Montgomery's face, he wasn't going to be happy about it, either.

"There is an explanation," Ty said, his chest growing tight. "We've been had."

THREE HOURS LATER and too many drinks to remember, they'd each learned a lot about their respective families. Ty lived on a sprawling ranch with a big close-knit family while Dex was a doctor who managed a huge medical conglomerate with his grandfather.

Finally, Ty convinced Dex of the only reasonable explanation. Dex Montgomery was not only his brother, but his identical twin. They'd both missed their flights home, but neither cared. Dex had phoned his financial adviser to brief her on his change of plans, and Ty had phoned his family, then his neighbor Leanne, who'd planned to pick him up.

The stories of their parents' whirlwind courtship, marriage and tragic deaths matched down to the dates. Dex was told, as Ty had been, that he had no other family. Ty could just imagine his grandparents' reaction when his mother had married a banker's son. Dex had been told nothing about their mother. Ty had been told zilch about his father.

"What I want to know," Ty said, his tongue thick in his mouth, "is how the hell they decided who would take whom."

For one long moment they simply stared at each other. Ty couldn't believe his loving family had lied to him. An image of his twin nephews surfaced. They seemed to have a special bond; he couldn't imagine anyone separating them. Yet that was exactly what his family had done to him and Dex. His family had pounded into his head ever since he could remember the importance of family and togetherness. He'd always felt a part of himself was missing, yet they had torn him away from his identical twin and told him he'd died.

Would he and Dex have had a special bond if they had been raised together?

On the heels of that disappointment, he wondered what his life would have been like if the other grandparents had chosen him. Would he be a different man today? Would he wear suits and make his living crunching numbers, sitting in countless boring meetings like those he'd had to endure the past three days?

He shuddered at the thought.

Dex cleared his throat. "My grandfather—"

"*Our* grandfather," Ty corrected.

Dex frowned. "Yes, our grandfather Montgomery will go ballistic when he finds out we met. He likes control."

"You think he was behind the separation?" Ty asked.

Dex nodded. "One-for-me, one-for-you—that sounds like his kind of scheme."

"So what do we do now?"

Dex drained his glass. "We should show up together and stage a confrontation."

Ty grinned. Both their families deserved to be shaken up. "You may have something there. I say we give 'em a taste of their own medicine."

A flash of concern darkened Dex's Scotch-hazy eyes. "What do you have in mind?"

Ty motioned to the waitress and then pointed to their empty glasses once more. "I'm talking about trading places, brother. For just a little while," he added quickly. "Just long enough to teach our families a lesson. And we'd get to meet the other side of the family." Ty had to admit he was curious about the Montgomerys. And his father. Maybe meeting them would help him feel closer to his dad.

Dex hesitated at first, but finally a smile slid onto his face. "Yes, that's good. All we have to do is bring each other up to speed on how to act and what to do." He flared his hands and inclined his head in a gesture of nonchalance. "It's simple on my end. You leave the business decisions to the old man. I have a secretary and a financial adviser who take care of things at the office. They'll keep you straight on the day-to-day schedule." Dex paused. "If a problem does come up and you need to make a financial decision on your own, just use your own discretion. After all, technically you are a Montgomery, too."

Only in blood, Ty thought. He had nothing in common with those ritzy people. Family meant everything to him. Money meant nothing, except it was a necessary evil, he reminded himself, if he was going to help his grandfather.

"What about the Coopers?"

"You shouldn't have any problems, either," Ty assured him. "Between Chad and Court and the ranch hands, they can handle things at the Circle C. It'll be good for both of us. We can get to know the other side of the family."

Dex nodded. "All right, then. I guess I could use a little rest and relaxation in the country. Kick back and get away from the grindstone."

Ty chuckled. He thought ranching would be restful? Hell, his brothers would probably wear him out. "Yeah, and I'll enjoy sitting on my butt in the air-conditioning for a change."

Dex laughed. "We have ninety minutes before the next flights leave for home," Dex said. "Let's do it."

Ty folded his arms across his chest. "You go first. I have a feeling your folks are a lot more complicated than mine."

Dex ordered another round of drinks. "All right. Here's everything you need to know in order to be Dex Montgomery."

# Chapter One

Jessica Stovall had cold feet.

Not in bed, as her ex-husband had once said, but cold feet about meeting Dex Montgomery. She was seriously considering turning her car around and heading as far away from the Atlanta airport as possible.

Had she actually volunteered—no insisted—she'd pick up Dr. Montgomery from the airport?

She must be a glutton for punishment.

Her 1985 VW Bug hit the curb as she parked in the short-term parking area, and she coasted backward, wincing when the gears ground together. She parked on a slight incline, then removed the rock from the floorboard and placed it behind the front wheel to keep the car from rolling. Someday, she had to get that emergency brake fixed. Her ex-husband had wanted her to sell the car a long time ago. But Nellie had been with her forever.

Just as she'd once thought her husband would be.

Only, Nellie hadn't let her down the way he had. A hollow emptiness pulled at her, the old pain resurfacing. He had left her when she'd needed him most. She kept Nellie because she needed to know something was constant in her life, that she wouldn't lose everything.

She hopped out, crossed the busy crosswalk, dodged a taxi and stumbled into the baggage-claim area where Dr. Montgomery's financial adviser had told her to meet him. This morning she'd knocked on his office door, hoping to beg him to reconsider his decision about funding the new children's wing at the hospital, but the doctor's gorgeous assistant, Bridget Holmes, had greeted her with a cool smile instead. Bridget was supposed to pick up Dex, but she planned to call a limo service for him. Jessica had jumped at the chance to give him a ride. Since she'd gone out of her way to make a trip to drive him home, he'd have to feel indebted to her and listen to her spiel.

At least she hoped he'd listen.

Dex Montgomery, doctor turned entrepreneur, was a shrewd businessman and seemed to have a heart for nothing but stock dividends and flow charts.

Jessica was the opposite. She loved her patients, the children at the hospital who needed tender loving care along with medical treatment. And she intended to see that they received the best of both. After all, the kids were her family now. The only one she would ever have.

She couldn't let them down.

According to Dr. Epstein, she had only two weeks to get the money, too, or the plans for the children's wing would be cut off completely. Besides, there were a few children who desperately needed money for treatment now.

Gathering her composure, she straightened her suit jacket and searched the crowd flooding the baggage-claim area for Dr. Montgomery. She was a respected pediatrician, a woman who'd risen from poverty to make a good life for herself by caring for others and keeping them from suffering. She refused to let Dex Montgomery intimidate her or reduce her to a jittery female.

His six-foot-plus, Armani-clad self would appear any second. All she had to do was play nice, dig deep enough to unearth his compassionate side and ask him for money.

Piece of cake.

Yeah, right.

Facing a firing squad might be easier than getting money from a Montgomery.

A DEEP SENSE of panic mushroomed inside Ty as the plane coasted to the runway. Two hours and a few drinks ago, this trading-places idea had sounded like fun.

But now his beer-induced bravado had worn off and reality had hit with the force of a two-by-four.

This charade was a mistake.

He should get off the plane and book a return trip to Bozeman. And fast.

The plane screeched to a halt, rolled to the gate, and when the seat-belt sign dinged, impatient passengers flooded the aisles, obviously anxious to return to their lives.

His stomach twisted. He should be getting back to his life—in Montana. Mending fences and herding cattle. Trying to figure out a way to improve things.

Not playing dress-up in this uncomfortable suit and choking tie. How did Dex stand it?

Because he'd never known anything else.

An ache, soul-deep, settled in Ty's chest. Somewhere in midair, he had contemplated what his family had done to him and to Dex, and his shock had dwindled, turning into anger and hurt. His loving grandparents, the ones who'd drilled into him his entire value system, had lied to him, had denied him knowledge of his own brother and his other grandparents.

He wasn't sure if he could forgive them.

Not only had they denied him knowledge about his father, but they'd robbed him of knowing his identical twin brother. What would his parents have thought if they'd known their boys had been split up after their deaths?

Maybe he would find out when he arrived, and maybe he'd learn a little about the man who'd fathered him.

And about why the Montgomerys had wanted nothing to do with him.

People rushed down the aisle, and Ty finally stood, reaching overhead for his beat-up duffel. Instead, his hand brushed over the soft leather garment bag Dex had shoved in his hands. He couldn't forget that damn briefcase, either. Dex had gotten so riled when Ty had almost left it in the bathroom after they'd exchanged clothes, a vein had bulged in his forehead. Apparently, Dex guarded the hunk of leather, along with his cell phone, as if they were his life. Ty scoffed. The bag alone cost more than he paid his ranch hands in a day. He wiggled his cramped toes inside the custom-made Italian shoes and almost tripped. The stupid shoes gave no support to his ankles. He certainly couldn't ride with them.

Of course, Dex didn't need a horse; he had cars and limos and taxis.

No, Dex had money. The kind that could have helped the Coopers.

But Ty didn't want their money. He simply wanted some answers about his past. The Montgomerys had given him up without batting an eye, and they'd written off Ty's sweet, loving mother because she was a rancher's daughter. Apparently they'd thought the Coopers weren't good enough. Just as Paula had thought he wasn't good enough for her.

The old pain haunted him.

*I could never live on a ranch,* she had said.

And he couldn't live anywhere else.

Besides, Dex seemed to have some strange ideas about his wealth himself. What was the last thing Dex had told him? *Be wary of everyone, especially the women. They all want me for my money.*

Ty could only imagine. No one had ever wanted him for his money. But he had certainly been exploited by a woman. Again, he thought of Paula. Just the sound of her name brought back bad memories.

Yes, he'd better be on his toes.

The ones that were now pinched and aching inside Dex's stiff Italian loafers. He slowly made his way out of the plane toward the gate. Thank goodness Dex's financial adviser planned to meet him in baggage claim. He'd follow her lead and let her show him the ropes. And when he met his other grandparents, maybe he would understand how they could keep one grandson and throw away the other.

JESSICA WRUNG HER hands together, trying to calm her nerves as she saw Dex Montgomery's tall, commanding presence rise above the crowd. The man was so darned good-looking he would stand out anywhere. His dark sexy gaze caught hers and a twitch of a smile actually pulled at the corner of his mouth, then he scanned the crowd without speaking.

Her stomach quivered, her pulse clamored and perspiration beaded her forehead.

She assured herself it was simply nerves.

She had too much riding on this project.

His chin lifted, and he strode right past her as if he didn't even know her.

Sure, he expected Bridget, but did he have to pretend she didn't exist? She called his name, fighting irritation, "Dr. Montgomery."

He continued looking across the crowd, oblivious.

She threaded her way between an overweight man and some teenagers until she stood behind him. "Dr. Montgomery."

He still didn't respond, so she gently caught his arm. "Dr. Montgomery, I'm here to pick you up."

His startled gaze swung back to her, a moment of heat splintering through her as he stared into her eyes. His ruggedly handsome face sent a flutter through her stomach, and his eyes were so dark they reminded her of chocolate kisses. She loved chocolate.

"Bridget couldn't make it," she said, shaking off the unsettling feeling. "Something about a business dinner. I offered to pick you up instead."

He stared at her as if he didn't recognize her, his thick dark brows drawn together. He'd let his hair grow, too, about a half inch longer than she remembered, giving him a rugged, primitive appearance. He probably wouldn't use an out-of-town barber, she thought, dismissing the slight difference and its effect on her. "Do you have more luggage?"

He shook his head, indicating the garment bag. "I carried on."

She nodded. "Come on, then. I parked in the short-term lot." He headed toward the MARTA sign and she frowned. What was wrong with him? He'd been in Hartsfield Airport at least a thousand times.

"It's this way." She laid her hand on his arm again. "Are you all right, Dr. Montgomery?"

He tipped his head and started toward the exit. "Yeah, just tired. It's been a long day." He ran a hand through his hair, a gesture she'd never seen him use. The movement spiked the ends, sending a lock over his high forehead. Somehow it made him seem vulnerable. "I fell asleep on the plane. I guess I'm not awake yet."

"Yes, I heard your flight was delayed." She led him through the doors toward her trusted VW. "Don't worry. I'll have you home in no time."

"You're sure you don't mind?" Worry laced his deep voice. "After all, it's awfully late for a woman to be downtown alone."

Jessica faltered, surprised by his concern. Maybe Dr. Montgomery really had a soft side hiding beneath that steel business veneer. "No, I don't mind at all. In fact, there's something I'd like to discuss with you on the way."

Trepidation filled her, but she gathered her courage. She'd just have to use the old trick her speech teacher in college had told her about— she'd picture him naked while she gave her sales pitch about the children's wing. Then she wouldn't be so nervous.

TY FELT NAKED without his Stetson.

Was that the reason this sexy little slip of a woman kept looking at him the way she did? Had he somehow already blown his new identity?

No, she couldn't possibly know.

Except he hadn't recognized her, and he obviously should have. But the noisy airport had his head swimming.

Who the hell was this knockout woman, anyway?

A coworker? Friend? Lover?

She was a little bitty thing, probably about five-three, and she had enormous grass-green eyes and auburn hair with flecks of red and orange that reminded him of a Montana sunset. Soft pink lips created a pouty little mouth that begged to be kissed, and the outline of her jacket showcased breasts that would just fit into the palms of his hands. Heat curled low in his belly, the pool of hunger undeniable.

Taking a deep breath to gather his control, he followed her through the dimly lit parking garage, his eyes feasting on the sway of her hips and the way that dark blue skirt framed her behind. She had shapely legs, too, as if she exercised regularly, although he couldn't imagine her wearing dusty jeans or doing hard work on a ranch, like the women he'd grown up with, the type of country girl he'd probably marry one day.

This woman was more like Paula. Educated, prissy, soft.

He'd learned his lesson dating a city girl a long time ago. Once burned, twice shy.

"My car's over here. I hope you won't be too uncomfortable, Dr. Montgomery."

A lover wouldn't call him doctor, would she?

"We'll just put your bag in the trunk."

She stopped at an old red VW bug, or what he guessed had once been red. The paint had faded, giving it a splotched effect, and the sunlight had turned the red to a dull orange.

He'd expected a limo, or Bridget to show up in an expensive sports car or Mercedes. Then again, he didn't really care. He was a humble guy himself.

His brother's words rang in his head. *Be wary of everyone, especially the women. They all want me for my money.*

This knockout had said she wanted to talk to him on the way home. Judging from her ancient car, she probably had financial troubles. Had she offered him a ride because she wanted money from Dex?

And if so, how far would she go to get it?

## Chapter Two

Ty wouldn't mind being seduced by her, he admitted silently. But he would never mix a relationship with business, especially with a woman like that woman.

Besides, Grandma Cooper would paddle his behind.

God, he missed her and the family. They'd probably be planning a welcome-home dinner for him right about now; he could practically smell the steaks sizzling on the grill and taste the buttery home-grown corn and biscuits.

Would the Montgomerys have a special welcome-home dinner, too? With Dex's favorite foods?

Worry knotted his stomach. He had no idea what Dex's favorite food was. How would he pull this off? Could he really pretend to be someone he'd just met?

What did he really know about his twin brother?

Nothing, except the information he'd crammed into his brain those few hours they'd sat in the bar. He and Dex might share the same genes, the same face, but they were completely different men.

He wanted to get to know his brother better. When this was over, he would.

The stunning auburn-haired woman next to him cranked the engine, then leaned outside the vehicle, removed a softball-sized rock from beneath her wheel and slid it behind the front seat.

"I have to get Nellie's emergency brakes repaired," she said.

He arched a dark brow. "Nellie?"

She nodded, a red blush creeping up her cheek to the auburn roots of her hair. "I named her in college." She patted the scarred dashboard. "We've been together a long time."

He couldn't resist a chuckle. Should he offer to fix Nellie's brakes for her? He was a decent mechanic; he'd fixed his share of farm equipment. Then again, did Dex know anything about cars?

Probably not. And if he did, Ty felt certain he didn't actually work on them. Dex wouldn't want to get grease on his expensive suits.

While the woman maneuvered her way through the parking-garage maze, Ty mentally reviewed the few things Dex had told him about himself. Dex had a medical degree, but he'd traded in his stethoscope for a computer. Now he ran a huge medical conglomerate called Modern Medical Maintenance, Inc., which he'd affectionately called M3I. As if a man could be affectionate about a medical empire, Ty thought. The company owned a chain of cutting-edge facilities throughout the Southeast that sounded as if they focused more on maintaining a profit margin than providing quality medical care.

Ty winced. Was he any better, though? He wanted more money to better the ranch.

Hell yes, he was different. He wanted to increase the ranch's profits so he could make life easier for his family. But he'd never take advantage of people's business problems or medical conditions to make a buck.

The VW hit a pothole, and he tried to adjust his legs in the cramped space, but his knees hit the dash and his head thumped the ceiling. The city air, the constant barrage of noises and the small space damn near suffocated him.

Oblivious to Ty's discomfort, the woman wove into the fast-moving traffic. Even this late in the evening, cars flew by as if they were racing in the Indy 500. Ty searched his memory for the woman's name. But Dex hadn't mentioned anyone specifically, except for Bridget, his financial adviser.

A car slowed in front of them and several cars blasted their horns. Ty held on to the seat as more horns blared, and a man in a van rolled down his window, shouting obscenities. Lord help them if these maniacs ever came to Rolling Bend and got stopped by a cattle crossing. Where was everyone going in such a hurry?

Buildings and billboards raced by, along with skyscrapers as they drove through downtown Atlanta. A million lights glittered from high-rise apartments and offices, obliterating the stars he might have seen in the Montana sky. How did these people live without fresh air?

"Dr. Montgomery," the woman began. "I know I mentioned this to you before, but I hope you'll reconsider giving me the money."

He gripped the seat edge. Maybe they did business like this in the city, but he was a Montana boy at heart. Sucking in a deep breath, he resorted to the pat answer Dex had told him to use.

"I'm sorry, Sugar, but all my financial decisions go through my adviser."

"Sugar?"

Judging from the tone of her voice, Ty had committed a cardinal sin. "Miss—"

"It's not Sugar *or* Miss," she said in a tight voice. "It's *Dr.* Stovall." She flashed him an angry look, then pressed her pouty lips together.

He fidgeted in the seat, feeling like a fish out of water, dying on the dusty ground. What the hell had he gotten himself into? At this rate, he'd be discovered before he ever met the Montgomerys.

So MUCH FOR being indebted, Jessica thought, fuming as she exited I-85 and veered through the Buckhead streets toward Dex Montgomery's estate.

He'd probably been offended by her car. Or maybe he thought she was foolish for being so tenderhearted she'd actually named her car Nellie.

Heck, why had she told him that little bit of trivia?

She'd just been so nervous, and for a minute, he'd looked at her as if he was actually attracted to her, as though he would really be interested in what she had to say, so she'd thought she'd seize the moment before it seized her, and she'd started babbling.

Darn it, she'd promised herself no man would ever affect her this way again. Hadn't she learned anything from her painful divorce? Jack had been a charmer, too. But looks didn't mean a man had character or that he could accept flaws in someone else.

She didn't even like Dex Montgomery; how

could she let him rattle her so? For heaven's sakes, he didn't even use his medical degree to help people; he'd swapped it for stock options and boardrooms.

No, it wasn't his potent sexuality. She was simply nervous because she'd hoped for his help in funding the hospital wing, and she had so much riding on his decision.

And he'd made the decision in a skinny minute without a single humane thought about whom he might be hurting. Why shouldn't he? The man had been born with a silver spoon in his mouth and had never wanted for anything, while she'd struggled for every scrap of education and every recognition she'd achieved. And those poor families and their sick children...

She stopped at the entrance gate to the long wooded drive of his estate and cranked her window down, refusing to apologize as the glass squeaked and squawked. Finally, she turned to Dex, confused at the baffled look on his face as he stared at the security gate. She was tempted to leave him here and make him walk up the drive.

Then again, maybe he was simply tired tonight, and tomorrow would be different.

Yeah, right.

Still, she pasted on a smile, forcing herself to be professional. "Go ahead, Dr. Montgomery, tell your security to let us through so you can get home to your family. I know you must be anxious to see them."

ANXIOUS WAS DEFINITELY the word, Ty thought, as he cleared his throat and tested his brother's name—*his* new name for the next week or so—"This is Dex, and uh, *Dr.* Stovall." He glanced at the doctor's face, hoping to see some hint of forgiveness for his blunder, but she stared straight ahead as if he didn't exist.

So, she was a doctor, albeit one with a rattle-trap of a car. That didn't mean she had to snub him.

He clenched his jaw, then realized he wasn't thinking straight. She couldn't be snubbing him because she had no idea he was Ty Cooper, Montana cowboy; she thought he was doctor/millionaire Dex Montgomery, and she was mad because he hadn't fallen into her trap and offered her money.

Remembering his mission for being here, his anger died. He couldn't get involved personally with her or anyone else because he'd be going back to Rolling Bend soon. Besides, when she found out who he was, she probably *would* snub him. Just as Paula had years ago. She was too educated to pay attention to the real Ty Cooper.

No, he wouldn't set himself up for that humiliation again.

She shifted into Drive again, the little bug spinning gravel as she bounced up the paved drive beneath an awning of trees that lined the entrance to Dex's house. It was too dark to see if the grass was green, but since it was May he supposed it would be. Thank God they had grass, and Dex didn't live in one of those downtown postage-sized, cookie-cutter condos surrounded entirely by brick and mortar. He thought of the rolling hills, the mossy green valleys and the dirt drive to the Cooper farmhouse and felt a pang of homesickness.

Seconds later, he forgot it as he stared in awe at the mansion in front of him. The houses they'd passed were big enough to be hotels, but this one reminded him of the governor's mansion.

How many people actually lived here?

Dex had mentioned his grandparents, a cook, a gardener, some kind of personal valet named George.

All people he didn't know.

Whereas back home he had his grandparents; his adopted brothers, Chad and Court; their wives, Jenny and Brenda; and their kids.

Dr. Stovall pulled into the circular stone drive in front of massive white columns and

Ty gulped. Would the people in this mansion be waiting for him with welcoming arms or would they recognize him as a fraud the minute they saw him?

## Chapter Three

Jessica watched Dex Montgomery unfold his long legs from the front of her car, grab his Gucci briefcase and his Louis Vuitton garment bag, and frowned. How many hospital gowns could she buy for needy kids with the money he spent on one piece of designer luggage alone?

Irritated with herself for obsessing, she glanced up and saw him staring at his house, the oddest expression on his face. He shifted on one foot, frowning as if his feet hurt, then turned to her.

If she didn't know better, she'd think he was dreading going into his own home.

He leaned into the still-open car door. "Thank you for the ride, Dr. Stovall."

So, he'd been trying to formulate a thank-you. Obviously a difficult task for him. Didn't he even thank his servants?

A small smile tugged at his lips. "I'm sorry if I offended you when I called you Sugar. It was just something I picked up on my trip."

*In Chicago.* Where? From one of his love bunnies?

She'd heard women fell all over him everywhere he went, but she didn't intend to be one of them.

"Forget it." She fluttered her fingers to wave goodbye. "I'll see you at the hospital."

His dark brows shot up as if he was surprised at her comment, but he quickly slid a mask over his expression. "I'm looking forward to it."

She nodded, then slid the car into gear and left him standing in his drive. Unable to resist, she checked her rearview mirror. To her surprise, his lips curved into a smile.

The damn man was flirting with her!

Dex Montgomery had never noticed her before; why would today be any different?

Had he undergone a personality transplant in Chicago?

TY WAS SURE he had blisters on his feet. Still, his aching toes couldn't compare to the hollow feeling he had inside as he opened the door to the Montgomery house.

Was Dex back at the ranch now, being embraced by his loving family? Would Ty get the same warm reception here?

A moment of conscience attacked him for

lying to the Coopers, but he shoved it aside. They had lied to him for thirty-two years.

It was time he knew the truth.

Time he met the other half of his family and learned about his father.

He opened the heavy mahogany door and slipped inside. The sound of his leather shoes hitting polished marble sounded foreign to his ears. The ornate entryway shimmered with soft light from the two-story chandelier, crystal tear-drops glittering like diamonds above him. He swallowed, listening for the sounds of family, laughter, kids, his dog. Of dinnertime. But only silence greeted him.

A cold empty silence that made him pause and analyze his surroundings. Elaborate oil paintings of the Civil War mingled with rich colors on the wall, leading to a double curved staircase covered in white carpet. Geez. He could picture his muddy work-boot prints on the steps, and Angelica and the twins romping around with sticky, jelly-crusted hands and muddy shoes. This place was nothing like home.

"Mr. Dex?"

Ty started and saw a stately-looking man dressed in a black uniform approaching. This had to be George, his personal valet, and according to Dex, his friend. His thick gray hair and stiff posture didn't look very friendly, though.

"We were expecting you earlier, sir. Long flight?"

Ty nodded. "Yes. Where is everyone?"

George automatically took the garment bag from him and gestured toward the right. "Your grandfather's in his study, as usual. And have you forgotten your grandmother always plays Bunco on Sunday nights?"

"Oh, right." What the heck was Bunco? They had a bunkhouse at home, but no game named after it.

"Mr. Dex, are you all right?"

"Yes." Ty scrubbed a hand over his face, suddenly weary. The less he said the better. "The trip, you know. I lost track of time."

George nodded curtly. "Very well. I wasn't sure if you'd eaten, but the cook prepared your favorite dinner. I'll bring a drink and your meal to your suite if you wish."

Ty stared at him in shock. The only time he'd ever been served on a tray was when he'd been sick as a kid. Gran Cooper had made him homemade vegetable soup with cornbread and let him stay in bed and watch cartoons. She'd played Scrabble with him. He doubted they had homemade soup and cornbread here. Or that they played Scrabble. Or that anyone would appreci-

ate the wood carvings he made. But his grandmother loved them. And Angelica had carried
the eagle he'd carved to show-and-tell. "No, I'll
eat at the table with the family."

George frowned again. "Sir, your grandfather
already dined, and your grandmother will have
hors d'oeuvres with the ladies."

So, no family dinner. "All right. You and I
can eat together."

George coughed, looking uncomfortable.
"Mr. Dex, thank you, but that's most inappro-
priate. You know I always take my dinner with
the staff."

Ty's stomach twisted. He was blowing this
big-time. George clicked his heels. "I'll have
your dinner waiting in the dining room in five
minutes."

He suddenly disappeared, his movements efficient. Ty shook his head in disgust; how was
he supposed to know how to act with servants?
At home, everyone joined in to help. They
cooked together, ate together and cleared the
table together. The men sometimes even washed
dishes. It was the Cooper clan way.

But he wasn't a Cooper here; he was a Montgomery and he had to act like one.

George would probably faint dead away if
he walked into the kitchen to help wash dishes.

No, he couldn't give Dex's personal valet a heart attack.

Was Dex having to learn to dress himself back in Montana?

Ty chuckled at the thought of his brother being that helpless and wondered how he would handle scrubbing pots at home. Would he have to clean the big cast-iron pan Gran Cooper used to fry chicken?

God, he wanted to get to know his brother better.

His stomach growled at the thought of Gran's chicken and homemade buttermilk biscuits, reminding him he was starved. Unsure where the dining room was located, he wandered to the right, trying to remember the tidbits Dex had mentioned. Dex's formal study occupied the first room, while his grandfather had his own private office upstairs off his suite. Apparently the house was so large they had separate staircases leading to their own wings.

Curious about his brother's office and hoping it would tell him more about his twin, he slowly walked inside, amazed at the fine leather and the rich woods of the furniture. Decorated in hunter-green and maroon, it was a masculine room that Ty might have felt comfortable in, except for the state-of-the-art computer system occupying the entire back corner. Two paintings of English hunt scenes hung on one wall flanking a brick fireplace that had obviously never been used.

Desperate for any information on his brother and his grandparents, Ty searched the desk and wall-to-wall bookshelf for family photos, but found none.

Odd. At home, his walls held dozens of snapshots of himself and his family members, of him and his neighbor Leanne. He wondered briefly what Dex would think when he met the girl next door, the girl the Coopers hoped he'd marry. He'd have to phone Dex and tell him to be nice to Leanne. She was just a sweet, innocent kid. He didn't want her to get hurt. She had enough problems keeping her own ranch going, especially with her ill mother.

Although both their families had been trying to push them together, he and Leanne had been friends forever, and he couldn't see her as anything other than a little sister. He was certain she felt the same way. Besides, he sensed that Leanne wanted to leave the ranch life for bigger dreams, and his life was home on the Circle C. Any woman he got involved with would have to love it, too. She would have to fit into his world of horses and cows and land. The ranch had been in the family for five generations; he wanted to make certain the legacy continued.

Dr. Stovall's vibrant grass-green eyes flashed into his mind, but he banished the image. Nope, that woman definitely belonged here in the city with fine museums and fancy hospitals and other doctors. Just as Paula had.

He definitely did not.

JESSICA COULD NOT stand to go home. The little house she'd rented near the hospital seemed too quiet and lonely since her divorce. The reminder of all she'd lost was painfully vivid every time she looked at the vacant room she'd painted as a nursery. Although she'd covered the bright yellow with a taupe color, when she looked at the walls, she still saw the room the way she'd imagined it during the first weeks of her pregnancy.

At the hospital she stared through the glass at the babies in the maternity unit, her heart aching. If she'd carried her baby to term, it would be a year old now. She would be planning a birthday party. She and Jack might still be together, a happy little family.

It was something she had never had, but something she'd always wanted.

Her hopes had been dashed when she'd lost their child, yet she'd tried desperately to recover. Then the doctor had delivered the final blow. She had severe endometriosis, and although she wasn't yet thirty, she'd had to have a hysterectomy. Traumatic as that had been, she'd tried to move on with her life, telling herself there were lots of needy kids in the world they could adopt.

At first Jack had agreed. He'd even been understanding and promised her it hadn't mattered.

But it had.

And eventually Jack had admitted it.

He wanted his own child, a son who would have the Thompson genes and carry on his name. Oh, he hadn't been ugly or mean; he'd simply been honest. Just the way he'd been when he'd told her to get rid of Nellie.

He didn't understand her sentimental attachment to the car. Maybe she didn't, either. But Nellie was the first thing Jessica had owned that had been all her own. And no one would take it away from her. She had worked damn hard to get that car and everything else in her life. She would get the money for these kids. Of that she was certain.

She wiped a tear from her eyes, smiled at the chubby little Rivers baby boy and squared her shoulders. She would not feel sorry for herself. There were children in the world, right here in Bethesda General, who were ill, who had to endure much worse suffering than she did. Children whose lives depended on expensive medical treatment; children who couldn't afford it—the very reason she was so disappointed in Dex Montgomery, the reason she would approach him again tomorrow at the board meeting when he wasn't tired, and she was prepared, her data and business plan in hand.

More determined than ever, she headed down the hall toward the pediatric unit. Late at night, she usually found some sick child lying in a hospital bed who felt frightened and alone. She would see who needed her tonight. Then maybe she could sleep when she finally went home. Maybe she wouldn't have nightmares of losing her baby.

And maybe she'd dream of a way to convince Dex Montgomery to help her.

TY STARED AT the massive mahogany table in the dining room in amazement. The entire Cooper clan could fit around it. Yet none of them would feel comfortable with the formal furnishings.

The dark maroon wallpaper reminded him of heavy drapes he'd seen at a funeral home. A crystal water glass that probably cost more than his grandmother's entire set of good dishes sat in front of him, and a short glass full of dark liquor—Scotch he presumed, since Dex had been drinking it at the airport—had been placed beside it. He reached for the glass and took a sip. A brush fire started in his throat, scalding his windpipe. Coughing, he grabbed the linen napkin, trying to hide his reaction when George slipped up behind him.

"Are you all right, sir?"

"Yea…yes. Thanks."

"Your salad." George handed him a plate of lettuce sprigs that looked like grass roots, followed by a saucer of something slimy.

Ty had no idea what the item was, but he didn't intend to eat it.

"Your escargot with risotto," George said, his shoulders thrown back with pride.

Escargot, Ty thought. Hadn't Leanne told him once that escargot was snails?

He didn't even eat cow tongue at home! Good grief, with the Montgomery wealth, they could certainly afford better grub. He'd starve to death if he had to eat like this. Irritated, he made a mental note to send Dex a freezer-full of prime hamburger and steak when he returned to Montana.

George stood stiffly by a long buffet, his body poised to jump to Ty's every need. "Aren't you going to eat, sir?"

"Um, I…was looking for the bisc…bread." *And the real food.*

"Certainly."

George returned with a basket of rolls, store-bought most likely, but at least Ty recognized them. Where was the butter?

He searched the table and saw a small china dish with pats of butter, so he slathered two pats on the bread. He inhaled it, only to catch George's eyebrows furrowed.

"Is something wrong with the escargot, Mr. Dex?"

*Yeah, it looks like it crawled out from under a rock.*

"Sir?"

Ty could have sworn the man's voice echoed in the huge empty room. How was he supposed to digest food, especially slimy creatures, with all this silence? Mealtime meant families talking and joking and arguing, rehashing the day on the ranch, kids throwing peas and clanging spoons, his dog Lady begging for scraps at their feet. After dinner Angelica would ride piggyback on his back; the twins would bounce on his knee. And sometimes he'd strum the guitar for a family sing-along on the porch under the stars.

Afterward, he and Pa Cooper would sit and talk—what did his grandfather Montgomery do after dinner? Sip brandy in his study and read his stock reports?

He pushed the plate of snails away and stood. "Sorry, buddy, but I guess my stomach's not up to speed tonight. I appreciate the supper, though."

George made a *tsk*ing sound as if he assumed Ty had drunk too much, then took the plate away. "Very well, sir. Shall I draw you a bath?"

Ty nearly choked on the roll. There was no way in hell he'd let another man draw anything in the bathroom with him. "No, thanks."

George nodded curtly, looking slightly offended as he rushed away with the plate. Ty grabbed two more rolls and stuffed them in the pockets of his suit so he wouldn't wake up with his belly so empty it was hitting his backbone, then left to find his bedroom. Poor Dex; how did the man survive on these piddly rations?

Still, he tried to look on the bright side as he climbed the steps in search of his brother's bedroom. Maybe tomorrow night he would be eating with the entire family and he'd learn more about them and his father. He'd be able to fool them better after a good night's sleep.

Dr. Stovall's face materialized in his mind—that was, if he slept at all instead of dreaming about that redheaded vixen all night.

Or if he didn't give himself away first.

## Chapter Four

Jessica woke slowly, a tingling sensation rippling up her arm all the way to her fingers. Slowly, she lifted the child snuggled next to her, slid her arm from beneath him, then flexed her fingers to rejuvenate the blood flow. Her watch read 5:30 a.m. They would be coming to prep Donny for surgery soon.

The three-year-old whimpered and opened his eyes. "Dr. Jesse?"

She gently pushed a lock of his blond hair away from his forehead. "What, sweetheart?"

"Stay till my mama gets here."

Jessica smiled. "Don't worry, I will." Donny's mother would come running in just as soon as she dropped her other two children at day care.

Then Jessica would have to run out in order to have time to shower and change before her eight o'clock appointments at her office. At eleven o'clock she had to break for her meeting with the hospital board. And Dex Montgomery.

"I scared," Donny whispered, fat tears pooling in his eyes. "What they gonna do to me?"

Jessica squelched the tears flooding her throat, knowing she had to be strong for the little boy, then began to explain one more time the scary surgery he faced. He'd been born with a hole in his heart, and the doctors had known they would need to operate eventually. They'd postponed it as long as possible. His prognosis looked good, but the surgery was costly, and his mother's health insurance minimal.

Patients like Donny were the reason she lobbied for more money for the children's wing.

"And when you wake up, your heart's going to be fixed, just like brand-new," she finished softly.

She only wished Dex Montgomery's heart defect could be repaired with surgery as well.

THE SOUND OF a knock woke Ty from a deep sleep. He flexed and rolled to a sitting position in his brother's big sleigh bed, surprised when he glanced at the clock and saw it was already 6:00 a.m. Geez, when had he slept so late?

Normally he crawled out of bed with the roosters.

He had to admit Dex's bed was comfortable, but he missed his feather pillows.

George opened the door and peeked in, a tray

laden with coffee and newspapers in hand. Ty's stomach growled, and he wished he had some bacon and eggs. He'd probably have that waiting downstairs. Maybe he'd get to eat with his grandparents.

He waited till George set the tray down before he wrapped the sheet around him and stood.

George stared at him with that pinched odd look again, as if he were wondering what planet Ty had stepped off. Dex probably walked around in front of the man in his underwear, but Ty did not get naked with other men. He was not shy, but he had to draw the line somewhere with this ruse.

"Your workout clothes are on the vanity in the dressing room, along with today's attire, sir."

Ty picked up the cup of coffee and sniffed. It smelled odd, as if it had some kind of flavoring in it, like the almond extract Gran Cooper used in her pound cakes.

"I know you must have missed your special brand in Chicago," George offered, his voice laced with pride.

Ty hated to offend him, but he could no more down the sweet-scented stuff than he could swallow those slimy snails the night before. "Actually," he began, clawing through his hair. God, he missed his hat. "I think we need to get diverse," he said, proud of his vocabulary. "I had some of that regular stuff in Chicago. Why don't you buy some today?"

George's brows furrowed. "Very well, sir."

Ty lifted the lid of a tall silver container.

"Your protein shake," George announced, implying it was his customary breakfast. "The cook added three raw eggs just as you like. Now, I'll leave you to your morning routine."

Ty grimaced at the thought of drinking raw eggs, wondering what his normal routine consisted of. At home, he'd eat a big breakfast, then work on the ranch till lunch with the sun beating down and the wide-open space calling his name.

His stomach growled again. "Oh, and pick up some good hamburgers and a steak or two while you're at it, George."

George's mouth fell open, but he quickly snapped it shut. "You aren't concerned about your cholesterol?"

Ty hedged. "I met with an investor who's working with the beef industry. Thought I needed to sample some before I give him advice." At least part of that was true.

George nodded. Apparently he understood business. "Hamburger and steak it is, Mr. Dex."

"And get enough for my grandparents tonight."

George halted by the door. "But, sir, they

won't be dining here this evening. They have plans at the country club."

Did they ever dine here? Ty wondered. "Well, *when* is the next family dinner?"

"I don't believe they have one scheduled this week."

They had to *schedule* family dinners? Now he'd heard it all.

"Your grandfather said you could ride in with him today if you want. He's leaving at eight-thirty sharp. Or you can drive yourself, if you want. The Mercedes is back from its grooming."

They groomed their cars? Ty almost laughed out loud but accepted the offer. At least if he rode with his grandfather, he'd finally get to meet him.

The man who hadn't wanted him or his mother.

Besides, he had no idea where his office was located or how to get there.


A FEW MINUTES LATER, Ty stood in the middle of a home gym that could have held thirty people. Everything in Dex's room and closet had been in order—even the gym was neat and organized—the opposite of how Ty lived at home. Gran would like that about Dex; she was always fussing at Ty to clean up.

He raised a skeptical eye at the equipment.

He'd considered skipping this part of Dex's routine but didn't want to draw suspicion to himself. Besides, he'd be relaxing the rest of the day, pushing paper behind a desk in some cushy air-conditioned office, signing his name, well, Dex's name, to a bunch of forms. He'd be so bored he'd be napping by noon. Might as well stay in shape while he was here.

He recognized the stationary bike from TV and the weights. An old buddy from high school had owned a set; he'd wanted to build muscles and impress the girls. He recognized the treadmill, too, from some guy demonstrating it on the tube.

He benched his weight for a few minutes, then climbed on the treadmill. Thank God George had unearthed some tennis shoes for him; they were a hell of a lot more comfortable than those Italian things Dex wore. He wondered if he could wear the sneakers with his suit.

Nah, they'd probably notice.

He fiddled with the knobs for a few minutes, trying to figure out the machine, when the surface beneath him began to move. Slow at first. Not bad. He walked with the motion, trying to adapt to the rhythm.

Piece of cake, although he'd much rather be outside riding his horse Dodger. Studying the different speeds, he punched a few buttons and the motion sped up. Faster, then faster, then faster. He pumped his legs and arms, increasing his pace until he was running to keep up, but the machine sped up, and he felt his feet sliding out from beneath him. Suddenly his shoestring got caught in the rung, his foot was being dragged tighter, closer to the edge and he thought his ankle was going to snap. He ran faster and faster, jerking his foot, trying to release it, but the motion continued, his toe came close to being ground in the machine and his chest was aching as he tried to breathe.

"Mr. Dex?"

George's shout alarmed him and he stumbled and lost the rhythm, then fell face-first against the bars. His nose hit the bar, his eye the handle. George rushed over and flipped off the machine. Ty struggled to breathe. Sweat poured off his body, his nose was bleeding and he thought he might have broken his toe.

"What happened, sir? Are you all right? Shall I call a doctor?"

The genuine concern in George's voice brought Ty out of his stupor. He could imagine his brother laughing his head off when he found out that Ty had almost killed himself on his treadmill. And *he* was supposed to be a doctor.

He wondered how Dex was faring on Dodger.

JESSICA HAD JUST finished her first round of patients when Dr. Epstein, head of the hospital board, phoned. Her nerves instantly jumped to alert.

"Are you ready for the meeting today?"

Jessica took a calming breath. She was as ready as she would ever be. "Yes. I have all my information together."

"I hope you can make this work. If we don't get an answer in two weeks, the plans for the new wing will be dropped. We've already gone through all the charity funds for this year." He hesitated, the sound of a pen clicking breaking the silence as he said goodbye.

Jessica hung up, thinking about the silent message behind his phone conversation. There were just too many families in need.

God, she ached for one of her own.

But if she didn't swing this deal with Dex Montgomery, all the families who needed assistance for the remainder of the year would be left without.

And their needs far outweighed her own.

TY HAD SHOWERED and shaved when George knocked at the bathroom door. Ty barely managed to wrap a towel around him before the door squeaked open.

"I took the liberty of calling your barber, sir."

George poked his head in and *tsk*ed again, then pointed to Ty's neckline. "I noticed your hair has gotten a little unruly while you were away."

He was probably thinking it wasn't the only thing that had gotten unruly, Ty thought. "Thanks. When do I go?"

George's eyes narrowed. "Your stylist is waiting for you in your suite, sir, as usual. He'll give you a trim before you go to the office."

Ty nodded and waited until George left, then yanked on the velour robe hanging over the door handle. He didn't know if he'd ever be comfortable having a man's man in his life, much less in his bathroom.

He grimaced. He was going to blow this if he didn't get his act together.

A few minutes later, he stared at the mirror in stunned silence. He had known he looked like his brother, but with his new haircut, he realized they were truly identical.

He wouldn't have known the difference between Dex and himself if he didn't know he was Ty.

But he *was* Ty, a Cooper, he reminded himself. A man who had always known exactly who he was and where he was going. A fifth-generation rancher who lived off the land.

Until he'd met his brother.

And learned about the Montgomerys.

Now, dressed in Dex's fancy suit and ties, he wondered if he would ever be that same man again.

JESSICA GRIMACED AS she hurriedly gathered her notes. The morning had been wild. Five ear infections, a four-year-old who'd stuffed a candy up his nose and a baby she'd had to put in the hospital for dehydration. Unfortunately, the three-month-old had lost the last of its fluids on her lab jacket. Thankfully, the formula hadn't soaked through to the suit she'd worn beneath, but the sour-milk smell lingered.

Dex Montgomery would not appreciate her new perfume. It wasn't exactly the two-hundred-dollar-a-bottle type he probably bought for his lady friends.

Her beeper chirped just as she reached the car. A moment of fear hit her when she read the hospital number. But she quickly jumped into Nellie and phoned the hospital.

"Dr. Stovall here."

"Yes, this is Dr. Blankenship. You wanted me to call about Donny?"

Jessica's breath caught. "Yes?"

"He's through surgery and holding his own for now. The next twenty-four hours will tell."

Jessica thanked Dr. Blankenship then hung up. She closed her eyes and said a prayer, then shifted Nellie into gear and headed toward the hospital for the board meeting. She'd stop by to see Donny and his mother after the meeting. Maybe she'd have some good news to tell them, that Donny's bill would be taken care of by some extra funds coming in, and that Donny's mother wouldn't have to lose her house to pay for her little boy's surgery.

Now all she had to do was convince Dex Montgomery and that barracuda business associate of his to help her.

Ty STARED AT his grandfather across the boardroom table, emotions churning through him. He'd hoped Grandfather Montgomery would embrace him when he'd met him at the car and he'd worried the older man would recognize him as an impostor, but his grandfather had simply nodded good morning, started his Cadillac and driven to the office. He'd barely even looked at Ty, much less noticed the difference. Ty should have been relieved, but he wondered if Dex and Grandfather Montgomery ever hugged or really talked about personal things. Whom had Dex turned to with questions when he was growing up?

Then Ty had noticed the pipe on the seat and made his first mistake; he'd asked his grandfather what kind of tobacco he smoked. Grandfather Montgomery had frowned and replied that Dex knew he'd given up smoking thirty years ago.

Was that the only thing he had in common with this grandfather? The fact that they'd both smoked at one time?

No, he and Dex had his dark eyes, as had their father. He remembered the photo album at home. Grandfather Montgomery had probably had thick dark hair, too, but now slivers of gray were threaded through the dark brown, and it had thinned slightly on top. He was a tall man with a commanding presence and a voice that spoke with authority.

Ty felt no real connection, and it bothered him immensely. Inside, something twisted. He wanted to impress the man, to get his attention and prove he was worthy of being a Montgomery. He fought the insecurities, yet he had felt the same way in those damn meetings in Chicago. And when he'd gone to the bank for the loan back home.

It was the same way he'd felt when Paula had published that stupid article about him. He'd met her when he was giving riding lessons at a nearby dude ranch when he was twenty-five. He'd fallen for her hard, only to find out later she'd been using him. Paula had returned to New York City and written an article for her journalism school, which had received an award and been published in a local magazine, complete with pictures, making him look like a clod with a run-down ranch. He'd not only been hurt but humiliated.

Did Dex feel this need to prove himself all the time? As if he had to win Grandfather Montgomery's respect?

Could Ty have inherited his drive to want more from the Montgomerys? Could that ambitious need be the reason Ty had always wanted to expand the ranch?

Had Pa Cooper recognized Ty's ambition as a Montgomery trait—was that the reason he was so strongly against it? Because he didn't want Ty to become like the Montgomerys?

Grandfather Montgomery stood. "I believe our meeting is over, gentlemen."

Bridget, Dex's financial adviser, curled slender, manicured fingers over his and smiled. Ty had immediately recognized her from Dex's description. Only, Dex had described her as efficient, brilliant, organized and attractive, while Ty's impression differed. She was a waif-thin woman with steel-gray eyes, short brown hair that resembled a man's cut and a voice that hinted of arrogance. He had no idea what his brother found attractive about her; she was so skinny a good stiff Montana wind would blow her over.

Had she and Dex been involved personally?

And why had his brother never mentioned Dr. Stovall?

"Thank you for coming," Bridget said, nudging Ty to stand. She shook each of the men's hands, and he followed suit. The two Japanese men owned a small medical building, which M3I had just purchased for a million dollars. He had listened to his grandfather crunch numbers, Bridget present flow charts, and he'd simply nodded, grateful they had things under control.

He had no idea what they had just said.

Was he ignorant compared to Dex? Uneducated—

"That was a steal," Bridget whispered.

For a million, the foundation must be built of gold, Ty thought.

"Dex, we have another meeting." Bridget's sharp high heels clicked on the floor. "The hospital board at Bethesda."

"Don't worry, it won't take long," Grandfather Montgomery added.

"Noes never do," Bridget said with a laugh. "I just hope that Jessica Stovall doesn't get emotional the way I've heard she can do."

Jessica…yeah, he liked that name. He could

imagine her getting emotional, passionate. Whispering his name in the dark…

"Dex can handle her," Grandfather Montgomery said. "Can't you?"

Ty nodded curtly, stifling the ridiculous fantasy.

"Come on, Dex." Bridget leaned over and whispered in his ear, "We'll ride over together and have some time alone."

A seed of worry sprouted inside Ty. What the hell did she mean—time alone? Were they involved? If not, did Dex want them to be?

"Uh, I'm riding with Grandfather. There's something I need to discuss with him," Ty improvised.

"We'll all ride together," his grandfather said in a commanding voice. On the way to the car, Ty struggled for something to say and prayed he wouldn't reveal himself on the ride over.

THE MINUTE JESSICA walked into the boardroom, her gaze latched onto Dex Montgomery. His dark eyes raked over her, a subtle look of hunger flashing in their depths. Seconds later, his financial adviser slipped so close to him a pencil couldn't be wedged between them.

Jessica shook her head. She must have imagined his reaction to her.

He was obviously involved with the barracuda.

Telling herself it didn't matter, she jerked her attention back to the hospital board, greeted each one in turn, shook Charles Montgomery's hand, Bridget's, then Dex's and pulled out her reports.

"We'll get right to the point," Dr. Sheffield, head of the board, said. "Dr. Stovall is here to present information regarding the new children's wing that has been proposed." He gestured toward Jessica.

*Picture Dex Montgomery naked. Picture him naked,* Jessica silently reminded herself. *Then you won't be nervous.*

She stared directly at him and saw his clothes disappear, his big, dark, broad shoulders being unveiled. Dark hair would taper down to his flat stomach, then V downward...

She shook the image away, disgusted with herself.

That image did nothing to calm her nerves. Picturing the sexy man naked only sent her blood pressure skyrocketing.

# Chapter Five

As the board meeting heated up, Ty jerked at Dex's boxer shorts, which had been riding up inside his pants leg. Thankfully on the way to the hospital Grandfather Montgomery had received a call on his cell phone and had lapsed into a business conversation the entire ride, saving Ty from conversation. He'd experienced relief at first, but by the time they arrived at the small hospital, annoyance had kicked in.

Pa Cooper had always been there to sit on the porch and talk to, listening to whatever problem Ty had faced throughout the day.

Everything except the subject of his father, he realized.

What if he really had wanted to discuss something important with Grandfather Montgomery? Did he have to *schedule* a conversation the way they did their family dinners? Was this the way Dex's life had always been, every minute thriving on mergers and acquisitions, with no time to talk about personal matters?

Jessica, no, *Dr.* Stovall, cleared her throat, and he jerked his attention to her slender legs and curvy body. With an air of confidence, she lifted a chart and listed the various programs needing funding and the financial requirements necessary to make them work. The terms and astronomical figures Ty heard made his head roll.

Ty had allowed Dex's financial adviser, Bridget, and his grandfather to bulldoze their way through the last meeting. He'd watched completely lost, as if he'd been dropped into a foreign country where everyone was speaking some strange tongue. He fully intended to let them do the same at the hospital board meeting as well. He could handle ornery bulls and the spring roundup of thousands of cattle, but the thought of making a decision about thousands— no, *millions*—of dollars involving life-altering medical procedures scared the bejesus out of him. At home, if a neighbor was in trouble, the surrounding ranchers pitched in to help. Here, they swooped in to take over the poor soul's company at the lowest price possible so they could selfishly sell it at the highest.

But Dr. Stovall's passion for her work intrigued him. He felt ashamed for the way he'd treated her yesterday. No wonder she'd been ticked when he'd dismissed her so curtly—he'd thought she intended to seduce him for selfish reasons, when she'd obviously wanted to plead with him to help sick kids, *her* kids she called them.

And although he'd never been a man who liked suits on women, her dark green one brought out the green in her eyes and hugged her body perfectly. He wanted to peel that suit right off. The jacket gaped open to reveal some lacy underthing that reminded him of the underwear he'd seen in a catalog Leanne had once received in the mail. He couldn't imagine his tomboy neighbor buying it, but his body hardened at the way the lace stroked Jessica's cleavage when she moved.

*Forget it, Ty. She thinks you're Dex. Besides, she's not your type.*

"These children need our help, gentlemen," Jessica said, dragging him from his lusty thoughts. "Without it some of them may not receive medical treatment at all."

His heart twisted at the agony in her eyes.

"There is funding in place," Grandfather Montgomery interjected. "The Montgomerys contribute to several charities that work with these families as well."

"It's not enough." Jessica's honeyed voice

rang with conviction, her breasts rising with her breath. "Bethesda Hospital is located in a low-income area and draws patients from transient families, immigrants and homes where most single mothers not only work at a minimum-paying job, but also have poor health insurance."

"That is their choice," Grandfather Montgomery stated. "We already provide one fund for those in need—we simply can't give out free services to everyone who comes crying."

Ty sat up straighter, his pulse kicking in at his grandfather's cold comment. Jessica Stovall's Irish blood roiled within her. Fire and worry blazed from those fiery green eyes.

"Most of these people are not crying for handouts, Mr. Montgomery. They're hardworking families who've fallen on hard times. Their children have been struck with diseases and illnesses that, unfortunately, require lengthy and sometimes extensive medical procedures, which cost an exorbitant amount of money."

"Dr. Stovall, we're aware of the problems," Bridget piped in, "but our company must also maintain a certain financial level in order to operate—"

"You're operating fine," Jessica snapped, sending a furious look at Bridget. "Your doctors drive fancy cars and play golf on Fridays while these children suffer."

Jessica yanked out photographs and began to spread them on the table. "Just look at this little boy. Donny is three years old and has a congenital heart defect. He underwent open-heart surgery just this morning."

Ty saw the faces of his twin nephews in the pictures, and his gut clenched at the thought of one of them undergoing something so frightening. The medical costs would virtually wipe out the Coopers' ranch.

"There's a child with leukemia who needs chemotherapy, and this little girl named Ashley was burned and needs skin grafts. Her parents died in the fire that injured her, so she has no one to care for her except an aunt with several children and financial problems of her own." Color darkened Jessica's cheeks as she became more impassioned. "Do you want to deny children chemotherapy or surgery, deny them the possibility of seeing another birthday or force them to go through life severely scarred so you can pay your doctors more or put a little more profit in your wallets?"

"Dr. Stovall," Grandfather Montgomery said sharply. "That is enough."

Ty snapped, "Yes, it is." He stood, placing both hands on the table, his eyes glazed as he stared at the precious children's faces. Jessica had spread out a dozen more photos, and he wondered what their stories were but couldn't bear to hear any more. He imagined how his family would feel if Angelica or the twins needed medical help they couldn't afford and no one stepped up to offer assistance. "You're right—these children are important. We'll find a way to make it work, Dr. Stovall."

Jessica's eyes widened in shock. Beside him, Bridget's surprised exclamation followed. He didn't look at his grandfather; he could feel his angry gaze scorching him.

But Ty didn't care. This was a no-brainer to him. What better use of the Montgomery fortune than to save the lives of innocent children? Surely, Dex would have agreed, wouldn't he?

JESSICA COULDN'T BELIEVE her ears. Had she just heard Dexter Montgomery override his financial adviser and his grandfather and agree with her?

He suddenly extended his big hand. "Maybe you and I can discuss the specifics later, Dr. Stovall."

"Yes, sure. Thanks." Jessica accepted his handshake, surprised at the rough calluses on his palms. Where had he gotten those? Did he have some hobby she didn't know about?

An inkling of a smile twitched at his lips, and she felt one forming on her own mouth. In spite of her reservations, heat curled in her belly, a dozen different sensations skittering through her at the dark look in his eyes. She couldn't flirt with the idea of a personal relationship— not after the pain of her divorce. She wasn't a one-night-stand kind of girl.

She'd also thought it would take a blowtorch to blast through his iron-clad exterior. Had he softened because of the children or because he wanted to add her to his list of conquests?

"I have to advise you not to meet without me, Dex," Bridget interjected in a biting tone. She indicated his grandfather, who slammed his briefcase closed with a decisive click. "We normally confer between the three of us before we close *any* type of deal."

"I said we'll work out the details," Dex said, cutting her off. "We can confer over the amounts later."

Bridget drummed her fingernails on the desk. "I can't possibly approve this—"

"I didn't ask you to approve," Dex said so curtly that Bridget actually took a step backward. Jessica almost chuckled, but the tension rolling off the senior Montgomery stopped her cold.

"I'll check my schedule," Dex said. "Maybe we can do lunch tomorrow."

Jessica nodded dumbly. "Yes, that'll be fine."

Dex's grandfather strode out of the office in a cloud of anger, Bridget on his heels. Dex lifted his hand to his head as if he was going to make some kind of gesture, then dropped it beside him, an awkwardness to his expression. "Until tomorrow, Jessica."

She nodded again. And she didn't realize until he'd left that he had called her by her first name instead of her title. He *had* meant a business lunch, not a date, hadn't he?

No matter, she would keep it professional. She wouldn't open her heart to any man, not ever again.

TY SHOOK HIMSELF, trying to dislodge the strange feelings that had overcome him when he'd shaken Jessica's hand. Hunger had bolted through him, a sexual craving he hadn't experienced in a long time.

Maybe ever.

He wanted to strip that suit off Jessica Stovall's curvy little body, touch that soft auburn hair, unwind it from the clip that held it at the nape of her slender neck and comb the long tresses down over her naked shoulders. Then he wanted to touch her everywhere, until she whispered his name in the heat of passion.

Only she would be whispering Dex's name, not his.

Reality slammed into Ty with the force of a concrete boulder.

He could not lust after Dr. Stovall—she led far too different a life for him to even think about becoming involved with her. He wasn't even the man she thought him to be; if she was attracted to him, it was because she believed him to be his twin—a millionaire doctor who could save her children, not a run-of-the-mill rancher with a few hundred head of cattle to take care of, a man who lived in the country where shopping consisted of a small general store and designer suits were nonexistent. Heck, he often smelled like cows and sweat and dirt, not expensive cologne.

No, getting involved with her would be all wrong, and sleeping with her was not an option. For God's sake, the woman thought he was his brother. And when Dex returned...

As soon as Dex's uncomfortable Italian leather shoes hit the hallway, Ty felt the tension emanating from his grandfather and Bridget. The elevator ride down lasted at least half a lifetime.

Dammit, he hadn't meant to be rude to his grandfather or Bridget, but how could they be so heartless as to turn down Jessica's—*Dr. Stovall's*—request?

"Don't ever override me again, Dex," his

grandfather ground out as soon as they had settled into his Cadillac.

"Or me." Bridget slammed the car door and crossed her toothpick legs, jiggling them up and down viciously.

"I didn't mean to override either of you." Ty hoped he hadn't messed up Dex's relationship with his grandfather. Grandfather Montgomery was the only family Dex had. Ty almost felt sorry for his brother. The Coopers would have welcomed him in.

"Then what the hell were you thinking?" Grandfather Montgomery bellowed.

"I was thinking about my n…" He caught himself, realizing he'd almost said his niece and nephews. And his twin brother. But Dexter Montgomery had no niece or nephews. "My need to help those kids," he improvised.

"Your need to help is admirable, son, but you seem to have forgotten the goals of M3I."

"And maybe we've forgotten that the needs of people should come first," Ty said, his own anger rising.

His grandfather clenched his jaw.

"What's gotten into you?" Bridget asked. "You've never let sentiment get in the way of a business decision before."

"That's right. The Montgomerys already donate to several charities," Grandfather Montgomery said. "And your grandmother hosts a ball for cancer research every year where we raise thousands of dollars."

Ty had no idea. Maybe his grandparents weren't so heartless. "I know, and that's great," Ty said. "But we can do more."

"And still improve our profits?" Bridget pinned him with her dark suspicious look.

"Yes," Ty said as confidently as possible. "I'll find a way to make it work, just watch."

His grandfather and financial adviser traded skeptical looks, then closed their mouths and didn't speak again the entire way back to the office.

Ty stared out the window at the neighboring high-rise buildings and silently vowed that he would find a way to make it all work. He couldn't disappoint Jessica.

No, not Jessica, he reminded himself.

*Dr.* Stovall.

As soon as Ty made it back into Dex's plush office, he searched the desk for a calendar to check his—Dex's—schedule for the day. Surely, he didn't have to face more of these stressful meetings. But he didn't see a calendar anywhere in sight.

Bridget walked in and shut the door. "Dex, can we talk?"

Ty froze momentarily, silently ordering himself to act nonchalantly—she couldn't have discovered the truth about him yet. Could she?

"Ye...yes, but first can you tell me where my calendar is?"

Bridget pointed to a little computerized thing in his briefcase that resembled a calculator. "In your Palm Pilot, where it always is." She narrowed her eyes at him, skinny arms crossed. "Now, why don't you tell me who you are and what you've done with the real Dex Montgomery."

# Chapter Six

Ty's stomach twisted. One day at the office and his financial adviser had already figured him out. Or at least she'd figured he was a fraud.

Would she tell everyone? Would they learn the truth before he even got to meet his grandmother Montgomery?

Panic gnawed at him. He'd hoped that if the Montgomerys got to know him as Dex, that once they discovered the truth, they would accept him as Ty. Then he and Dex could bring the whole family together.

His grandmother Cooper always told him he was a dreamer.

"Dex?" Bridget tapped her fingernails along his desk.

"What...what do you mean?" he asked.

"I mean you've forgotten your Palm Pilot. In fact, you've been acting weird ever since you returned from Chicago. You haven't looked at your schedule all day. You waltz into a business meeting, go soft and offer to cut profits for charity, you disagree with your grandfather, and—" she smiled seductively "—you haven't acknowledged all the hard work I've done while you were gone."

Relief spread through Ty, along with trepidation.

So, she hadn't totally figured out the truth.

But he had no idea what sort of thank-you she wanted—business or personal? Dex hadn't said they were involved, had he? "You know I appreciate you, Bridget."

He searched his memory and cursed himself for drinking so much beer when he and Dex had been talking. But he'd been so shocked to learn his twin was alive...

"I always knew you were a good man, Dex, and I admire your great mind, but you're usually much more practical when it comes to business." She laid a friendly hand on his arm, and Ty smiled, pretending the gesture was just that—friendly. If she and Dex were involved, it wouldn't be right to touch her. Not that he wanted to anyway.

No, if he touched anyone it would be Jessica Stovall.

And that absolutely could not happen.

Dammit, he felt as if he was sinking into red mud and had no one to throw him a rope.

He slowly extricated himself from Bridget's hand. Bridget poked pouty lips outward, then turned and sauntered to the door. "Now, get that business head back on, Dex. I've missed you. Just think what the two of us can do together with this company."

With a flirtatious wink, she opened the door and flitted out into the hall.

Ty clawed his hand through his hair. He had to ask his brother about that woman. Did Dex plan to include her more in the running of the company? And if so, did his grandfather Montgomery know their intentions? Had he planned to retire soon and let Dex take charge of things?

JESSICA TRIED TO forget about Dex Montgomery's luncheon invitation as she raced into the hospital. The lunch was strictly business, nothing personal. Exactly the way she wanted it.

Didn't she?

She paused to grab two cups of coffee from the hospital lounge, then found Donny's mother in the waiting room and slipped a cup into her hand. "How are you holding up, Diana?"

The young woman looked exhausted, but she smiled and hugged Jessica. "Good. They say Donny came through surgery fine, that he's a real trooper."

Jessica patted Diana's back. "Well, we both know that. He takes after his mama."

Diana beamed. "Thank you for staying with him last night. I wanted to be here." The woman choked on her emotions, and Jessica rubbed slow circles on Diana's tense shoulders to relax her.

"I was happy to be with him. I know Frankie and Jean-Ann needed you last night. They must have been frightened, too."

Diana nodded. "We all slept together and said a prayer before I took them to the sitter."

Jessica thumbed an errant strand of Diana's shaggy brown hair behind her ear. "It looks like God was listening." In more ways than one, Jessica thought, remembering Dex Montgomery and the handshake that had confirmed their deal—and his change of heart. Excitement lacing her voice, she proceeded to tell Diana about the wonderful doctor who had promised funding to help pay for Donny's surgery. A brief memory of her own son flashed in her mind, the loss aching as always. She only wished she could have carried him to term, that he'd had a chance.

But at least Donny had a chance now. Thanks to Dex. Dex Montgomery had definitely returned from Chicago a new man, and she liked the changes she'd seen so far.

She just hoped the old one never returned.

THE REST OF THE DAY had passed in a blur of boring business meetings, most of which Ty had endured, letting Bridget and his grandfather run the show.

He had to or he would give himself away.

Back in his office he stared at the computer files and blinked to clear his vision, the glare of the screen making his head pound. Sure, he'd sweated on the ranch, but something about all these high-tech financial equations gave him the jitters. The muscles in his neck were knotted like a rope, his nerves stretched tauter than the fencing he used to hold the cows inside.

To think he'd believed Dex's job was easy, that he'd be napping by noon. Geez.

After studying the Montgomery files, he'd learned much about the business. He knew the number of medical buildings M3I owned, the number of takeovers they'd managed this year, the goals of the company, the names of various stocks and investments his grandfather held, that his grandfather trusted Bridget and that she was a cutthroat financial maniac.

He vaguely wondered what she would say about the way he kept his books on the ranch. Granted he had tried to keep up with the times and had splurged for a computer to house his financial records, but his record-keeping was primitive compared to the Montgomerys. The memory of Paula laughing at him surfaced. She would have liked Dex.

Dex had education and money.

Once again, his pride smarted, but he tried to dismiss it, reminding himself that he didn't need a doctoral degree to run a ranch. He needed common sense, a strong body, a good work ethic and knowledge of the land and cattle. All of which he had.

How was Dex surviving?

He had to find out. Maybe tonight he could sneak in a phone call.

A knock on the door jerked him from his thoughts, and he shut down the files just before his grandfather poked his head in.

"I'm having dinner with the mayor tonight. His driver will be here shortly so you can take the car home."

Ty nodded, instantly thinking of home as the Circle C.

His grandfather dropped the keys on the desk, then paused to study Ty, his dark eyes narrowed. Ty squirmed, wondering if somehow his grandfather suspected the truth.

Instead, he said, "I hope you're figuring out how to deal with Dr. Stovall and settle this extra-funding issue, son."

Ty chewed the inside of his cheek. Did his grandfather expect him to back out on the deal?

Well, he'd better not hold his breath.

Coopers were men of their word.

"You'll do the right thing for all of us, won't you?"

Damn right. He'd help those needy kids. He remained silent, though, simply nodding.

His grandfather smiled, obviously convinced Dex had come over to his way of thinking. "Good. I knew you would, son. After all, you are a Montgomery."

Ty's chest squeezed as his grandfather closed the door. He was half Montgomery, yes. But he was also half Cooper. And so was Dex.

Only, they'd each been denied the other half since birth.

The unfairness of it all burned through his belly. The birthday celebrations they'd missed together, the Christmases, the camping trips he'd loved so much. Would Dex have enjoyed those? And what would Dex think of Ty's woodworking?

Ty palmed the car keys, suddenly anxious to leave the high-rise building. He only hoped he could remember how to get back to the Montgomery estate.

Then he'd search for something that told him about his father. Maybe he'd finally meet his grandmother, too.

He hoped she'd give him some idea why the

Montgomerys hadn't wanted anything to do with the Coopers. Then maybe he could figure out how to bridge the gap between them.

A HALF HOUR LATER, Ty had managed to maneuver through the traffic and pulled up to the security gate of the Montgomery estate, but his nerves bucked back and forth the way they had the first time he'd ridden a bull in the county rodeo.

All because he was going to meet his other grandmother.

It had been too dark when he'd arrived the night before for him to notice the beautiful landscaping of the estate, the small pond to the side of the property, the way the mansion was perched at the top of a grassy hill like an antebellum mansion from *Gone with the Wind*. Though the estate consisted of less land than his thousand-acre ranch, it probably cost a fortune. Just as he approached the house, Dex's cell phone rang. Ty fumbled with it, praying an investor wasn't calling needing specific information Ty wouldn't be able to give him.

But Jessica Stovall's soft feminine voice purred over the line. "Dr. Montgomery, this is Dr. Stovall."

"Hey, Jessica. Call me Dex."

She hesitated, and he wondered if he should

have used her title, but he couldn't bring himself to apologize. "What can I do for you?"

"I...I wanted to verify our lunch plans for tomorrow."

"Sure. What time is good for you?"

He pulled the car into the garage, yanked out Dex's Palm Pilot and toyed with the buttons, trying to find Dex's schedule while he waited for her reply.

"I should be free around one. Can we meet someplace near the hospital? I'd like to check on Donny and his mom during my break."

"Sure. Maybe I'll go with you."

A soft surprised sound escaped her.

Ty gritted his teeth. Had he screwed up again? "Something wrong?"

"No, no, that would be great. It might be nice for you to meet some of the kids on the wing, so you can see where your money will be going."

Where Dex's money would be going, Ty thought, praying his brother wouldn't mind. And if he did...well, he'd figure out something. The one nice thing about having money was being able to give it to kids and people like Jessica Stovall.

Then again, maybe he should avoid her. No sense flirting with the impossible. "Look, if it's a hassle—"

"No, no hassle. I think it's a good idea," Jessica said. "I really do think you'll feel good about the funding when you see these kids, Dex."

What could he say to that? "It's a date, then," Ty said. "One o'clock. You can give me a tour first, then we'll grab some lunch."

"Great." Jessica paused, her breath whispering over the line. "And, Dr. Montgomery—"

"Call me Dex."

"Well, okay, Dex. Thanks. You won't regret this."

Jessica said good-night, then hung up. Ty thought of his grandfather's reaction to the deal. No, he wouldn't regret offering the money, but Dex might not be so happy about what he'd done. Oh, hell. His brother was probably creating messes at home that he'd have to straighten out when he returned. And Dex had told him to use his discretion if a problem arose.

But he would regret it if he got involved with Jessica. Besides, he would be leaving soon—he didn't want to go back to Montana with a guilty conscience. He had enough troubles and responsibilities at home without adding a woman into the equation. Especially a city woman who wouldn't fit into his lifestyle.

No, he wouldn't think about her. He'd focus on the Montgomerys—the reason he'd come to Atlanta in the first place.

He tucked the cell phone and Palm Pilot back into Dex's treasured briefcase, climbed out of the car and went inside to meet his next challenge—fooling his grandmother Montgomery.

## Chapter Seven

When Jessica hung up the phone, her emotions were boomeranging between happiness over the funding and caution over any kind of personal relationship with Dexter Montgomery.

Of course, he might not have a relationship in mind at all.

But he had sounded slightly flirtatious on the phone, and he had called their meeting a date.

No, it couldn't be a date. Jessica Stovall did not date. Not since Jack had walked out on her. Not since she'd lost everything. She would never open herself up to that kind of pain again.

Her tabby cat, Twinkles, purred and rubbed up against her, and Jessica scratched her behind the ear, grinning when the cat followed her to the bathroom. Twinkles dropped onto the furry rug while she removed her clothes, dropped them in the hamper and slipped into a bubble bath. It didn't matter if Dex was interested in her, she reminded herself; she was not interested in him.

Not as a man anyway.

No matter how sexy and appealing he could be. No matter how much money he gave to the kids. No matter how much he made her heart race and her blood boil.

She sank deeper into the thick bubbles and closed her eyes, relaxing as the warm water sluiced over her. Unbidden images of Dex floated into her subconscious. She could see him standing in the bathroom doorway, sliding off those Italian shoes, peeling off his jacket and tie, slowly unbuttoning the small white buttons of his shirt, then tossing it onto the hamper beside her clothes. A shiver trembled through her.

His broad shoulders reminded her of a linebacker's, and his arms and chest had been sculpted like an athlete's. The dark hair on his chest would taper down his washboard-flat stomach and V into those slacks. He would peel those off as well, and she would see his thick muscular thighs and legs.

Then she would whisper his name, beckoning him to join her, and his eyes would blaze with heat. Her nipples beaded beneath the bubbles, a warm languid heat spreading through her at the idea of him climbing into her bath. She wanted to invite him to do more.

She jerked her eyes open, heat flaming her cheeks, perspiration trickling down her neck. Embarrassed at her wayward thoughts, she quickly washed and toweled off, pulled on a robe and let the water drain from the tub.

Her fantasy drained from her mind just as quickly.

Dex was a Montgomery. His family prided themselves on having the best of everything. She didn't fit into that category. She wasn't the best woman or even a whole one in the way that counted most.

A dull ache gripped her as she walked toward her bedroom, and she paused to stare at the empty room that would have been her baby's nursery. Unable to help herself, she went inside, hesitating beside the box of baby paraphernalia. She kept meaning to give the items to Goodwill, but the thought of parting with the baby things had been so painful.

Jessica reached inside, picked up a small yellow teddy bear and hugged it to her chest. Her hand automatically covered her stomach, and tears welled in her eyes. Tears for all that could never be. For the son that she'd lost, and the hopes and dreams that had died with him.

If she did get involved with Dex, it wouldn't last. He might not ever want marriage or kids. But if he did, he would no more want to adopt than Jack had. No, the Montgomerys were proud of their name and their place in the city; they wouldn't accept an heir that didn't have their own blue blood running through him.

And even if she could have children, Jessica Stovall did not have an ounce of blue blood in her. Her own mother had worked as a hairdresser in a small shop called the Cut and Curl. Her father had run off with an exotic dancer from the local strip club when she was two.

Jessica had always longed for a big family, for sisters and brothers to laugh and play with, but her mother had never remarried, so Jessica had spent her days alone while her mother worked to make ends meet. Her mother's drinking and chain-smoking had finally gotten the best of her, and she'd developed emphysema. Jessica had felt so powerless to help; she'd taken her toys and dolls and turned them into patients. Patients she could heal because she hadn't been able to help the one person in her life who mattered.

Her mother had finally died when Jessica was seventeen. Since then, she'd been on her own.

Except for her brief marriage to Jack.

That first year she'd been sure she'd finally have that big happy family.

But it wasn't meant to be. She'd misjudged Jack and maybe jumped into things too quickly.

Another reason not to jump into anything with Dex.

She ran her finger over the carousel music box the nurses at the hospital had given her when she'd first discovered she was pregnant, then wound the stem and listened to the soft music of "When You Wish Upon a Star." Twinkles came in and purred at the music, and she smiled sadly. Her wishes for love and family were too foolish. Hugging the bear to her chest, she let the tears fall, wiping them away angrily with the back of her hand and mentally wiping away those lusty images of Dex Montgomery.

There were children that needed her as much as she needed them. And she would not let a sudden case of sexual attraction distract her from her goals.

Why was she suddenly attracted to Dex Montgomery, anyway? She never had been before, and she'd seen him and talked to him dozens of times. But yesterday, he'd been so different. It was as if she'd met him for the first time.

It didn't matter. She carried the bear to her bedroom and laid it on her pillow, vowing it would be a reminder to keep her head on straight and off Dex Montgomery's strong, handsome shoulder.

She'd always heard that Dex didn't mix business with pleasure. Tomorrow, they would meet for a business luncheon, and if he had other ideas, she'd remind him of his own philosophy. She'd had all the heartache in one lifetime that she could handle.

"YOUR HAMBURGER, SIR." George cleared his throat as he set the plate in front of Ty.

Ty's mouth watered.

Although the food looked better, he grimaced at the silence in the room. He was still eating alone at a table that could hold twenty.

"I believe it's prime U.S. beef. The butcher said he gets it from somewhere in Montana."

Ty cut his gaze toward the elderly man who was supposed to be Dex's friend and thought he detected a slight grin tugging at George's mouth. Had he guessed Ty's secret?

"Ketchup and mustard are on the table. And the cook prepared baked beans to go with the hamburger." George's frown seemed pinched. "She said they're often served together."

Ty's stomach growled. He reached for his fork, then remembered that Dex was right-handed instead of left-handed. He'd probably wind up spilling beans all over Dex's suit if he tried to eat them with his right hand. And George was watching him as if he was way too suspicious. "I think I'll take this outside and eat it. Do you have any paper plates?"

George's eyebrows shot up, his eyes squinting in disgust as Ty drenched the fat burger in ketchup. "I suppose I could find one." He reached for the dish. "Your grandmother just arrived from the country club. I believe she's on the veranda, by the pool."

Ty's appetite waned, his excitement and nerves kicking in. He figured the veranda was the porch, so he headed through the house to find it while George hurried off in search of paper products. He couldn't imagine being a kid here, playing in the dirt and dragging in worms and fish. Or that snake he'd caught to take to school to scare the teacher with the last day of seventh grade.

The floor was so clean and shiny, you could eat off it. He'd bet the housekeeper here worked her butt off. He wandered through the hallway and opened the double French doors leading to a brick patio. Shrubbery and hanging ferns created a garden effect surrounding the pear-shaped pool. Huge magnolias and oaks were scattered through the property, dogwoods blooming their delicate white petals and dropping them to the ground like snowflakes. A bar stood to one side, equipped with liquor and an ice bucket; a wrought-iron table complete with an umbrella for shade occupied the right corner. Next to it, Ty noticed an ornate white gazebo draped in roses and a path cutting toward a greenhouse.

The fresh outdoor air smelled like sweet clover, reminding him of the clean skies and countryside in Montana. A moment of homesickness attacked him, but he brushed it aside the moment he saw his grandmother Montgomery sitting in a chair beside the gazebo.

Emotions he hadn't expected welled in his throat. He stuffed his hands in his pockets and stared at her, wanting to enjoy the sight of her before she spotted him. She seemed small, almost fragile in size, but regal-looking with soft gray curls that feathered around her oval face. The age lines etched around her eyes added a hint of wisdom to her angular features, and her silky-looking pantsuit made her look elegant. Silver shoes and diamond stud earrings completed her simple but stately outfit. The diamonds were most likely real, he realized, remembering how Gran Cooper had shrieked and cried when the boys had chipped in to buy her a pair of fake diamond studs for Christmas last year.

Gran Cooper probably appreciated hers more than this lady. He shook himself, regretting the thought. He didn't know Grandmother Montgomery. He shouldn't judge her before he'd even talked to her.

His resolve kicked in; the smile came naturally as he approached her.

"Gran...mother," he said, remembering the title Dex had given her. "How are you?" He automatically bent and hugged her as he always did Gran Cooper. He hadn't realized how much he'd missed physical contact since he'd been here.

She lifted thin arms and embraced him quickly, almost awkwardly as if they didn't hug very often, patting his shoulder. "Hello, son, what's gotten into you?"

Ty grinned, grateful she hadn't minded his display of affection. He'd needed to hug her, to know that this woman was real, that she really loved Dex.

That maybe she could love him as well when she learned the truth.

"I just missed you, that's all," Ty said quietly.

Her pale green eyes twinkled with a smile. "Well, then you'll have to go to Chicago more often. It's not like you to be so affectionate."

He rubbed the back of his neck, praying he hadn't already been pegged for a phony.

"So, how did your meetings go in the Windy City?"

"Fine," Ty said, hoping to avoid business. But he was hungry for anything more about family. Of course, he couldn't just come right out and ask her all the questions bombarding him, either. "What have you been up to?" he asked.

His grandmother sipped her iced tea. "We've been organizing the annual mother-daughter tea at church. This year we're doing a fashion show—the benefits go to the women's circle and their mission this summer." She waved an age-spotted hand, gold and diamonds flashing in the fading sunset. "Then again, you're not interested in hearing all this women stuff."

Ty cleared his throat. "Of course I'm interested, Gran...mother. I always like to know what the Montgomerys are up to."

She laughed softly, the sound as musical as wind chimes. George approached, carrying a thick paper plate loaded with Ty's hamburger and baked beans, along with a pitcher of tea. He set it on the umbrella table, a skeptical look of apology aimed toward Grandmother Montgomery.

"Thanks, George."

George nodded. "Let me know if you need anything else."

Ty waved him off. "Everything looks great."

"Are you really eating red meat?" Grandmother Montgomery's voice wavered with surprise.

Ty clenched his jaw. These folks acted as if beef was pure poison. It provided vitamins and minerals and was full of protein. "Yes, I met a stockbroker in Chicago who tried to rope... talk me into investing in beef. Figured I'd try a little out myself."

She wrinkled her eyes as if she didn't quite buy his story but couldn't pinpoint what exactly was wrong with it, either. He rushed on to keep her from thinking too much.

"The roses look great."

"They do, don't they?" A proud smile lifted her lips. "But I'm most proud of my African violets. You should see them—they're in the greenhouse."

"I'd like that," Ty heard himself say as he wolfed down part of his meal.

His grandmother tilted her head sideways. "You want to see my violets?"

"Well, sure." Ty chewed, wondering if Dex had never expressed an interest in his grandmother's hobbies or life before. Of course, he assumed she had a gardener or someone who tended the garden; she probably didn't do it herself.

A few minutes later, she surprised him. "I usually come out early in the mornings to tend to them," she said as she led him down the path to the greenhouse. She paused to point out several varieties of flowers on the way. Ty didn't know their names, but he did appreciate the fact that she enjoyed the outdoors and that she liked to grow things.

Gran Cooper had a green thumb, too. She loved her vegetable garden and would tinker for hours, pruning and tweaking the small section of herbs and flowers she grew.

Why couldn't his two grandmothers have been friends?

His grandfather's voice boomed behind Ty as he approached. Had Grandfather Montgomery kept the Coopers and Montgomerys apart or had everyone wanted it that way?

## Chapter Eight

Ty had no idea how to find the answer except to stage a confrontation.

He wasn't ready to do that yet.

He needed to get to know the Montgomerys better. Remembering all the times he'd worked with wild horses, he told himself he had to be patient. He had to weave his way into this family so they would accept him when the time came to disclose the truth.

He wondered if Dex had learned anything on the ranch.

Now might be a good time to call home. His grandfather and grandmother Montgomery had taken a stroll together in the gardens. At home, the Coopers would be finishing with supper so everyone would be busy with cleanup or with the kids.

He carried his paper plate into the kitchen, ignoring the odd look from the cook at the sink and George as he dumped it into the trash. His manners intact, he reached for his hat to tip it and realized it was missing. That he was not Ty. He was Dex. But surely Dex was polite.

"Thank you, ma'am. That was a mighty fine supper."

George grinned and the cook's chubby cheeks puffed up into a smile. "*Sí,* Mr. Dexter. I am glad you enjoyed."

Ty rubbed his stomach. "I'm looking forward to the steak."

Well aware George's eyes had narrowed, his focus scrutinizing Ty as if he was trying to pick him apart, Ty slid past him, then went to Dex's office and roamed through it, studying the books on the wall-to-wall built-in shelves. He didn't know what he was looking for, but he needed to find something in this house that might give him answers. And tell him about his family.

He finally spotted it. A gold-embossed photo album.

Gran had tons of albums at home; one entire album dedicated to his mother. The book also held a picture of his mother and father together at their wedding. His parents had looked so young, so happy, so in love. So hopeful for their future.

Had there been other pictures at home; ones of his parents with him and Dex? If so, had his grandmother purposely removed them so he wouldn't learn the truth about his twin? That he was alive, living across the country?

An emptiness pulled at him. Somehow he just couldn't reconcile his loving family as people who would do such a thing. But it had happened. Meeting Dex was all the proof he needed.

He took the album to the desk and opened it, his chest tight as he saw his father's face fill the pages. The baby pictures made him laugh. A photo of his father's first day of school followed. Ty's throat closed as he realized the similarities in looks between his father and him. And Dex.

He flipped the pages and saw more shots— his father earning some school awards; he'd obviously attended a private school nearby. His father in high school on the tennis team, the debate team, winning a science award. Graduating from high school, college and medical school.

He had nothing in common with his father. Ty had played baseball, horseshoes, ridden in the local rodeo. He'd done poorly in biology, although he'd enjoyed agriculture. His grandparents had always told him he was like his mother; that they both had a way of communicating with the animals.

Then again, his father had been raised in a different world. As Dex had. He studied the pictures again, looking more closely this time.

In each photo, his father looked so solemn. So intent and serious.

Unhappy.

Not at all like the smiling young man he'd been in the wedding photo with Ty's mother. Pride filled him as he realized that his mother had put the smile on his father's face. She'd given him happiness and love, two things his solemn, studious, workaholic father had obviously needed.

But he didn't find a single photo of his father and mother together in the Montgomery album. It was as if they refused to acknowledge that part of their son's life. But why? Hadn't they seen how happy his parents were together?

How would his father and mother have felt if they'd known their sons had been separated? Had they anticipated a family feud over the boys and stipulated the separation in their will? Somehow, he doubted it...

More torn than ever, he closed the book and placed it back on the bookshelf.

Deciding not to use the office phone in case his grandfather walked in, he hurried up the long staircase, grabbed the phone in his room and ducked inside the huge bathroom. Feeling like a kid trying not to get caught with his hand in the cookie jar, he punched in his home number. His nerves jangled as he heard the phone ring; if anyone besides Dex answered, he'd have to disguise his voice.

On the third ring, a carbon copy of his own voice sounded over the line. Dex. Thank God.

"Ty?"

"Yeah, it's me."

"Why the hell didn't you tell me about the investors and the chaps? And…Leanne," his brother muttered in a hoarse whisper.

"Me? Why didn't you tell me about that piranha you've got working for you? And I think George is suspicious!"

"What?" Dex asked, sounding confused. "What piranha?"

"Bridget whatever-her-name-is," Ty snapped. "Are you two involved?"

"No, I don't mix business with pleasure, although sometimes I think she'd like it if we were together." He thought he heard Dex chuckle. "Tell her you want the monthly status reports early. That should keep her busy for a while. My best advice would be to avoid her if you can."

As if he wasn't already trying to do that.

"What about George?" Ty demanded. "How do I handle him?"

"Tell him you're not in the mood to discuss it if he starts prying. That usually does the trick. What about your investment meeting?" Dex prodded.

"There's nothing to tell." Ty relayed the fact that he'd been trying to expand the ranch and improve profits, but Dex had apparently already learned that. "You'll get an official response within a few days. Let me know the moment you receive it. I'm anxious to know which way the wind is going to blow."

"All right. And you let me know how it goes there."

"Will do. Anything else? I don't know how much longer I can hide in this bathroom. George may be spying on me as we speak."

Dex chuckled. Damn him. He was probably eating up the Coopers, in more ways than one. Those homemade biscuits with honey…Gran's hugs. His brothers'.…

They were Dex's brothers, too.

"One more thing. About Leanne."

"What about her?"

"I thought you told me you were just friends."

"We are," Ty said flatly. "I guess I forgot to mention that our families would like it other-wise."

"I guess you did," Dex retorted drily. "And this dance?"

"The one on Friday night? It's just a fund-raiser. I take Leanne every year just to keep the peace in the two families. Little bit of square-dancing, foot-stomping." Ty imagined Dex trying to buck-dance to "Duelin' Banjos" and grinned.

"I guess I can take her," Dex said slowly.

Ty chewed his cheek. Surely, his twin hadn't taken a liking to sweet little Leanne. She wasn't his type. Then again, she was pretty and young. Damn Dex. "You'd better be nice to Leanne. And behave around her," Ty warned. "She's young and innocent, and I don't want her hurt in all this."

"Neither do I," Dex said.

"Good. Now, how's my family?"

"The Coopers are fine," Dex said pointedly. "They're waiting for me to join them outside."

Ty closed his eyes, a small spark of something like jealousy skittering through him. But guilt slammed into him, replacing the jealousy. He couldn't be territorial about the Coopers. They were Dex's family, too, and the Coopers always had room for one more.

At least he'd thought they had until he'd learned they'd made this agreement with the Montgomerys.

In his mind, he saw the big family gathering around the TV for popcorn and a movie. The kids, the laughter, the noise. He loved them and missed them.

But he had liked his grandmother Montgomery, too. Sure, he didn't know her that well, but he could see a softness in her eyes, a spark of true affection. He would have known that affection sooner had the Montgomerys and Coopers not separated the boys.

And Dex would have been a part of the Coopers' lives. Then they wouldn't be having this conversation. In fact, he and Dex might have been friends just like he and Chad and Court. They would have shared both families. And a lot of good times together. Would they have competed in sports?

His mind drifted to Jessica—would they have had the same tastes in women?

"Ty, I gotta go."

"Okay, but one more thing." Well, really two. He had to ask about the money. "What's between you and this Dr. Stovall?"

"Dr. Stovall?" Dex paused, seconds ticking by. "Nothing. She's a pediatrician at the hospital. Sort of a do-gooder—"

"There's nothing wrong with that."

A long sigh punctuated the silence. "Listen, Ty, watch your step. I have to come back there, remember?"

Ty nodded, even though he knew Dex couldn't see him. "Don't worry. Everything's under control. Only there—"

"Listen, man, I gotta go. Angelica's on my heels."

Dex hung up and Ty grimaced. He still hadn't asked about the money.

Oh, hell. Dex had told him in the beginning to use his discretion. He was worrying for nothing.

Besides, he wanted to prove to the Montgomerys that he had some business sense himself. That he could move the numbers around, make this deal work and still clear profits for them.

Maybe he wanted to prove something to himself, too. That when he returned to the ranch he could solve those problems as well.

In the morning, he'd review M3I's financial situation and the funds Jessica had suggested. After that, he'd meet Jessica for lunch and work out this business deal.

Then his grandfather would have to admit he was worthy of being part of the family. After all, he wasn't Ty Cooper, cowboy-rancher, here in need of money. He was Dex Montgomery, doctor, businessman, head of one of the largest medical conglomerates in the U.S. He had resources at his fingertips that he could use for some good. And he intended to do that before he returned to his own world.

After all, Ty Cooper had nothing to offer Jessica Stovall or her children. Irresistible as she was, he'd be a fool to start something as Dex— not only would guilt eat him alive, but he'd get burned in the end when she found out the truth.

She probably had a ton of men after her anyway. What would she want with a rancher?

THE NEXT DAY, Jessica hurried up the hospital steps, grateful she hadn't had any emergencies. She desperately wanted this meeting with Dex Montgomery to go well. Then she could get the money she needed and be done with the handsome doctor. Her poor heart couldn't stand the torture of that man firing up her hormones with his too-charming smile and voluptuous mouth.

A smile and mouth she'd never noticed before he'd returned from Chicago. Whatever had happened to the man there, she certainly hoped the change stayed with him permanently.

In fact, if her memory served her correctly, before his trip, he'd stalked through the hospital corridors with a frown on his face. Always rushed, always hurried, always concerned with crunching numbers, never taking time to notice her or any of the staff, much less the children.

But today he wanted a tour, and she intended to give him one. If little Ashley Torry didn't steal his heart, no one could.

Which was fine, because Jessica had no intentions of letting him near her heart.

He was waiting at the nurses' desk on the pediatric wing when she arrived. Jessica sucked in a sharp breath. In a couple of hours, the deal would be sealed, and her business with Dex over with for good.

THE MINUTE TY saw Jessica he knew he was in trouble. She beamed a smile at him that reminded him of sunshine and late-night picnics by the lake. He wanted to touch her so badly he had to stuff his hands in the pockets of his Armani suit. Her gaze met his, and he shifted, pulling at the confounded tie and wishing he could take it off.

Damn, his brother had more suits than a clothing store. He'd fully intended to choose his own clothes this morning, but he'd taken one look at Dex's closet—it was as big as the upstairs bathroom at home—and gotten dizzy. Then he'd pulled out a few ties and shirts and tried to match them up, but George had walked in and taken pity on him.

He wondered what Jessica thought of George's selection. Even worse, he wondered what she'd think of him in dusty jeans and his Stetson.

What the hell was he thinking?

She would think he was a down-on-his-luck rancher who smelled like cow dung and dirt.

"Hi, you're right on time."

Thank God she hadn't been able to read his mind. "Yep. I'm ready for the tour."

Jessica nodded, the miniature Big Bird attached to her stethoscope bobbing up and down.

He reached out and touched it. "Cute."

She blushed. "Sorry, I was in a hurry. Forgot to take it off." With a small laugh, she pocketed the instrument. "Come on. I'll show you my pet project."

He resisted a flirty comeback and followed her down the hall, feeling oddly out of place as she spoke to the nurses on staff. Her title, *Dr. Stovall*, was a great reminder of why he was there, that he and Jessica belonged to two different worlds. That this lunch date had everything to do with M3I and her kids. That he had a ton of responsibilities back home waiting for him.

The hospital had been built about fifty years before, Jessica explained, but they kept updated equipment, and the staff consisted of top-notch doctors, some coming from Atlanta's own prestigious Emory University. Being so close to the facility also allowed volunteers and student doctors to train there, which helped with patient load and enabled more individual care.

"Your office is here?" Dex asked.

Jessica shook her head. "No, there's a medical building adjoined to it where I see patients daily. Patients needing emergency treatment or referrals to specialists go through here. I also help out here when the staff is short."

"That doesn't leave much room for a social life, does it?" Dex asked.

Jessica bit down on her lip and led him into the children's rec room. "No, but that's okay with me. My life is here with the kids."

Dex caught her arm. "Your whole life, Jessica?"

Jessica pulled away, uncomfortable with his probing look. She didn't want to answer personal questions at all. Obviously sensing her unease, he backed off.

"So, this is where the patients come for fun?"

Jessica chuckled. "As much fun as they can have in the hospital."

"I'm sorry. I didn't mean to imply—"

"It's all right," Jessica said. "I wasn't chastising you, Dr. Montgomery."

"Dex."

She sighed. "Dex. But yes, we provided this room for parents to read, play games or do other quiet activities with their children while the kids are recovering. As you know, depression is a major problem with illness and affects recovery. Keeping children stimulated helps promote a positive attitude."

Dex nodded. "Of course."

"We want to expand the facilities and include some computers for games, even access to the internet for patients to do short school assignments while they're here."

"That sounds logical."

She continued to point out different programs they hoped to implement. "And now, the best part."

The door opened and a crew of nurses and nurse's aides helped several children inside the room. Some came in wheelchairs, some with walkers; others walked but pushed an IV pole; one rail-thin boy who'd lost his hair from chemotherapy walked in with a football clutched to his chest.

Jessica's heart squeezed at all the brave little faces. When she glanced up, she was surprised to see the compassion and concern in Dex's eyes. He didn't speak, only smiled at the children. A little girl with jet-black hair named Molly dragged a beloved blanket behind her, her gait made awkward by the braces supporting her legs. Suddenly her brace caught on the end of her blanket and she pitched forward.

Dex moved in a flash, gently swooping her tiny body into his arms. "Whoa there, little lady. You were about to take a magic carpet ride."

Molly giggled and clutched Dex's broad shoulders, laughing when he slowly eased her back down to stand. The airplane noises he made when he lowered her caught all the kids' attention.

Jessica laughed, unable to believe her eyes. The kids all yelled at once.

"I want to ride, too."

"Me, too."

"Me, 'free."

Dex shrugged. "I'd love to, you guys, but I think the doc here has something else planned for you." He paused to stoop down and speak to each child individually. When he came to the little boy with the football, he patted him on the back.

"When you get better, son, let me know, and we'll go outside and throw that ball. I bet you'll have an arm on you like Joe Namath."

"Who?"

Jessica laughed as he explained the legendary football hero, her throat nearly clogging with emotions. She'd thought Dex Montgomery didn't like kids; she'd never imagined he'd actually be good with them. But he had a kind, sensitive side. He would make a wonderful father...and he was so damn attractive. It would be easy to fall for him.

At least for the Dex Montgomery she'd gotten to know the past week.

But if he married or had children, she reminded herself, his kids would be Montgomerys. And she would have no part in it. Her hand automatically went to her stomach, the deep emptiness squeezing inside her again like a vise.

"Hey, you guys, it's story time," the head nurse announced, quieting the group.

The small children settled around a big rocking chair, and an elderly woman wearing a big cape and carrying a bag of puppets took the center of the small stage. One last child slowly entered, wheeled in by a young nurse's aide.

"That's Ashley," Jessica whispered. "She's the little girl who needs plastic surgery."

A muscle worked in Dex's jaw at the sight of the pale child. "Where's the little boy you mentioned—Donny?"

"He's still in ICU. He's not ready to be around the other kids yet. Too much risk of infection."

Dex nodded. "And the story lady?"

"She's a volunteer," Jessica whispered. "I contacted one of the local churches, and we organized a program to get their senior citizens involved with the kids. The older people were bored and lonely, so it's been great for everyone. And the kids love the attention and time together."

Dex folded his arms across his massive chest, his voice rough. "I've seen enough."

Jessica stiffened. "Did you change your mind about helping us?"

Dex cupped her elbow with his hand, sending a dozen sensations skittering up Jessica's spine. His dark gaze pierced her to the core. "I never go back on my word, Jessica. Now, let's go someplace private so we can talk."

Jessica's heart fluttered in her chest. They were only going to talk about the center, she reminded herself.

Which was exactly the way it had to be.

## Chapter Nine

Jessica eased into the corner booth at the small Italian café where she and Dex had decided to have lunch, her senses on overload. The booth was secluded, the room dark, the smell of wine and marinara sauce overpowering. As was the man she was having lunch with.

Watching Dex with the young children before they'd left the hospital had completely touched her heart. He had promised them he would come back and visit, agreeing to read them a story when he returned.

She had never imagined Dex Montgomery would be a sap with kids. But he had been putty in their creative little hands. And when he had hugged little Ashley goodbye, she'd thought she'd even seen a tear in his eye. She'd definitely had one in her own.

Pushing aside her foolish thoughts, she studied the menu, trying desperately to distract her racing pulse and her pounding heart.

"Would you like a drink?" he asked. "A glass of wine to seal the deal?"

Jessica shook her head. "No, thanks. I have more patients to see this afternoon." Besides, she didn't need wine; her head was already spinning.

The waitress arrived with water, and Dex ordered spaghetti and meatballs. She bit down on her lip, surprised. She could have sworn one of the nurses had mentioned he didn't eat red meat.

"I'll have the spinach stromboli." She handed the menu to the waitress and glanced up to see Dex watching her. Knowing she had to remain professional, she launched into a discussion of the hospital. When their food arrived, they fell into a companionable silence. It was too easy being with Dex, Jessica thought, too nice, too comfortable, too…too titillating.

Her body thrummed with a strange kind of heat and a yearning that seemed to be growing out of control.

She had to deny her feelings. Didn't she?

"I've been looking over M3I's financial situation this morning—I have a few more files to review." Dex placed his napkin on the table. "Then I can let you know an exact amount."

"Thank you, Dex." She squeezed his hand, wanting him to know how much this project and his support meant to her. "I can't tell you how excited I am. This is going to help so many children. Did I mention we're going to build a therapeutic playground in conjunction with our physical-therapy program?"

"That's wonderful." Dex snapped his fingers. "Let me be your first volunteer to help build it."

Jessica had to struggle to contain her reaction. Dex was full of wonderful surprises. "You'll really work on it?"

"Of course. It'll be fun." He caught her hand again, twining their fingers together. A flood of sensations rushed through her. His dark eyes seemed almost black in the dim light, and the flicker of candlelight gave his tanned skin an almost bronze appearance, reminding her of a cowboy riding across the prairie at dusk.

"What? Do I have food on my face or something?" He rubbed the shadow of his beard.

"No, I was just wondering how you stayed so tanned when you work inside all the time." *And thinking about how handsome you are, and how much I want to touch your jaw.*

He shifted, his gaze darting down to his silverware. "Uh, tanned. I don't know."

She had to keep the conversation light. "Playing golf, huh?" Jessica asked, enjoying the slight blush on his face.

He shrugged. "Guess you caught me."

Jessica laughed. "I imagine you're pretty good. You probably play a lot."

"Uh, not as much as I used to. I'm changing my priorities."

"You are, aren't you?" Jessica said softly. The warmth of his palm seeped into her, sending all kinds of delicious sensations through her. She told herself she should pull away, yet a tingle rippled through her at the hunger in his eyes, and she couldn't bear to release his hand. Instead, she curled her fingers into his and met his gaze.

His cheeks grew uncharacteristically red. "Yeah. I want to do good things with the Montgomery money."

"Thank you for coming to the hospital today." She fidgeted. "And I'm sorry we got off on the wrong foot when I picked you up at the airport."

"That was my fault," Dex admitted. "I... So many people approach me because they want something—"

"Money, you mean?"

He nodded. "Yeah, I guess I've gotten wary. So much that I shut you out before I heard what you had to say. I'm sorry."

"I'm just glad you did finally listen," Jessica said softly. "This project means everything to me."

"Don't you have room for a man in there somewhere?"

Jessica sipped her water, the pain of her first marriage splintering through her. "I did once," she admitted, her throat thick. "But I'm sure you heard about my divorce through the hospital grapevine."

"I don't listen to gossip." He arched an eyebrow. "Are you still in love with your ex?"

Jessica's gaze swung to his. "No…I'm not in love with him," Jessica said, realizing it was true. She and Jack had dated while she was in med school, and they'd sort of fallen into marriage. Then the pregnancy…

Come to think of it, she'd never really dated anyone else. She hadn't been experienced at all and had probably been swept up just because he'd paid attention to her.

Something she wouldn't do again.

"I'm sorry. I didn't mean to stir up old hurts."

She forced a smile. "Water under the bridge."

"Really? Then why no other man?"

"Because I've been too busy with work, the kids, trying to get this new wing started."

"You have to stop and smell the roses sometime."

"Is that what you've decided to do, Dex?"

The question seemed to catch him off guard. His fingers tightened around hers. "Maybe. But I want to take care of my family, too."

"Your grandparents?"

A muscle ticked in his jaw. "Yes. What about you? Where's your family?"

"Gone," Jessica admitted.

"All of them?" Dex asked in a gruff voice.

Jessica nodded, staring at their joined hands. He had large knuckles, big fingers, calluses, strong hands.... She didn't want to let go. "My father left my mom and me when I was two. My mother raised me alone."

Dex grew quiet. "I'm sorry. I guess you were close growing up."

Jessica shrugged. "She worked hard to raise me, but she..." How could she tell this man that her mother hadn't been educated? That she'd drunk too much and smoked too much, and that Jessica had pretty much raised herself. That even so, she'd still felt lost without her when she'd died. That she'd desperately wanted a family of her own...

"Jessica." He gently lifted her chin with his other hand, the contact so soft yet intimate that Jessica shivered. When she looked into his eyes, she saw concern and tenderness and a hunger unlike any she'd seen from a man.

His masculine presence offered strength and comfort, things she hadn't had in a very long time. Without thinking about the consequences, she slowly brought her fingers up and touched his jaw, traced a finger over the rough stubble she'd wanted to touch earlier and down to his mouth.

He caught her finger and pressed it to his lips and kissed the tip. Then, with a low groan, he angled his head, cupped her face in his hands and brushed his lips over hers in the sweetest torture she'd ever known.

Ty knew he should have stopped himself, but he was so caught up in the moment, he couldn't help himself. He'd already known Jessica was a spectacular woman, a great doctor, but he'd never guessed that underneath all that care for others beat a wounded heart.

His was hurting as well.

Because he wanted her to know that she was kissing Ty Cooper, not Dex Montgomery. What would she do if she knew? Would she hate him for lying to her? For deceiving her?

Would she even *like* the real Ty Cooper?

He hated being dishonest. Coopers had good values; he'd never lied to a woman or used one before in his life.

But he had never tasted anything as sweet as Jessica's lips. Guilt warring with desire, he deepened the kiss, his hunger intensifying at her touch. She tasted like Italian food and sweetness and woman. And she smelled like roses. Hot, passionate and wild, just the way he'd imagined.

His fingers slid into her hair, tugging at the

clip that held it, and suddenly her long auburn tresses fell across his hand. A low moaning sound escaped her that sent adrenaline straight to his groin, and he shifted, moving closer to her to pull her into his arms. Her breath brushed his cheek; her hand curled on his chest, burning his skin through the fabric of his shirt. He wanted her to unbutton the buttons, to run her hands over his torso, to touch him everywhere. And he wanted to do the same to her.

But someone cleared their throat, rather loudly, and he remembered they were in a public place.

Would Dex have behaved so boldly?

He gently nipped at her lips, raking his tongue across them one more time before he eased away. Her eyes were closed, but when she opened them, he saw the dazed look of a woman struggling to control the passions within her.

He wanted to dance with those passions. To take her right there on the table.

What the hell had come over him?

He heard the throat-clearing again, and out of the corner of his eye, he spotted a tall beanpole woman with her skinny arms crossed, her lips pursed, her high heels tapping on the floor.

Bridget, Dex's financial adviser.

"So this is your business luncheon?" she asked tightly.

Ty grimaced. He'd made a mess of things all right.

But he refused to let Dex's right-hand woman tell him what to do. At least outside the office.

"Yes, we were discussing the new wing for the hospital," Ty said, the tension palpable.

Obviously embarrassed by their public kiss, Jessica's face had turned a thousand shades of red. Ty grimaced. She worried her bottom lip with her teeth, making him want to kiss it again, then brush more kisses on the slight abrasion on her cheek where his beard had chafed her. And he'd unfastened that clip in her hair so the beautiful tresses lay in a tangled web around her shoulders.

Damn. He'd *never* let a woman rattle his composure before.

She looked loved and all sexed-up, as if she belonged to him. He wanted to take her in his arms and finish what they'd begun.

Was he an idiot? A glutton for punishment. He'd only known the woman a few days. Hadn't he learned anything from Paula?

"I thought I advised you against that deal," Bridget said.

It took Ty a minute to steer his mind back on track. Oh, yeah, the business deal. "You did." Leaning back in the chair with a nonchalant attitude, he added, "But I've been looking over the books, and I think we can make it work."

"Is this how you close all your deals, Dr. Stovall?" Bridget cut her scathing gaze toward Ty. "And is she the reason you've been avoiding me?"

Jessica's mouth gaped open.

Ty saw red, but he managed to keep his voice a low, lethal tone. "That's enough, Bridget."

"I should go," Jessica said, suddenly standing.

Ty reached for her hand. "Jessica, wait." He angled his head toward Bridget. "Unless there's an emergency, I'd appreciate it if you'd leave us alone for a minute." He remembered Dex's advice. "And by the way, I need the monthly reports a little early. Could you work on those for me?"

Bridget gave Jessica a menacing look then frowned at Ty, turned and stormed away.

Jessica's fingers trembled as she released Ty's hand and tucked her hair back inside the clip. A few people had noticed and were staring, so he coaxed her to sit down and lowered his voice.

"Jessica, look, I'm sorry. Please don't leave upset. Let's talk."

"There's nothing to talk about, Dex."

Like cold water to a flame, hearing his brother's name doused any remnants of hope lingering from the intimate moment.

"We made a business deal, and we should leave it at that." She reached inside her purse for her wallet, but Ty glared at her, daring her to offer to pay, and she slipped it back inside. "Thank you for lunch. Just let me know when you come up with the final figures." She extended her hand. "It's a pleasure working with you."

He swallowed and shook her hand, knowing she was right to keep their relationship on a business level. He didn't like this attraction brewing between them—or want it. He had too much to do here and back home to get tangled up with her.

And he'd make sure when he saw her again that their relationship reverted back to the way it was before—strictly business.

JESSICA WAS MORTIFIED. Not only had she forgotten her vow to keep her arrangement with Dex professional, she had been caught making out with him in public by the barracuda.

The news would probably hit the hospital grapevine in nanoseconds. And when Dex moved on to another woman, as she knew he would, she'd receive those pitiful sympathetic looks. Poor Dr. Stovall. Why couldn't she hold a man?

She couldn't handle the gossip again.

She had to get herself under control—even if she wanted to tear Dex Montgomery's clothes off and make love to him right in the middle of town.

And even if her heart was begging her to trust him.

She hadn't trusted anyone in a long time.

As much as she hated to be the exact type of person Dex had described earlier, the kind that only wanted something from him—money— she had to stick to her resolve. Because money was the only thing she could take from him.

No more kissing Dex. No more touching him. And no more dreams of being in his arms.

TY COULDN'T STOP thinking about Jessica.

But he could not repeat that kiss. He was making too much of this infatuation anyway. His crazy behavior was probably a result of being out of his element. It wasn't as if he'd never kissed a girl before. Only it had been a long time. And there hadn't been anyone special since...since when?

Since Paula had made a fool of him.

He'd have to look around town when he got home. Maybe he could find a girlfriend at one of the dances. One who liked country music and country dancing and country life. Then he'd be laughing himself silly that he'd even entertained the idea of kissing a woman like Jessica Stovall. Chad and Court would probably laugh their asses off.

Determined to find an answer on the exact funding the Montgomerys could offer, he spent the afternoon studying the company's financial records, investments, debts and plans for future projects.

By five o'clock, a massive headache pounded at his temple, and his eyes were blurry from deciphering numbers. But he had found a few items he could trim from their budget, mainly champagne breakfasts and expensive gifts. There were a couple of smaller accounts labeled B & B. He made a mental note to ask Bridget about them.

He was thankful she'd buried herself in her office beneath the monthly reports and hadn't yet surfaced. Maybe he'd speak with his grandfather about the accounts tonight.

He also had an idea for a fundraiser he wanted to hash over with Jessica. He'd already phoned to talk to her about it, but she'd hadn't called him back.

He had a feeling she wouldn't.

With a long sigh, he turned off the computer. He intended to keep his promise and visit the hospital kids for story time tomorrow. According to the nurse he'd spoken with earlier, Jessica usually dropped in to visit around lunchtime. If he was lucky, maybe he wouldn't run into her. Then he could get a handle on his libido and put it back in its cage where it belonged.

And then he could focus on his plan, return to Montana and get on with his life.

# Chapter Ten

The next morning, Ty pulled on Dex's gym clothes, determined to master the treadmill today. After all, he'd ridden bucking bulls before and tamed wild horses; he could at least walk on a treadmill without killing himself.

Afterward, he would shower, speak to his grandfather and Bridget about those accounts and go to the hospital to visit Jessica.

Uh, no, to visit *the children*.

Seeing Jessica would be a nice bonus. A really, really nice bonus.

A knock sounded at the door, and Ty opened it, not surprised to see George.

"Sir, Ms. Bridget is here. She said you have a racquetball date."

*"What?"*

"She's waiting in the living room."

Ty scratched his head, panic streaking through him. He wasn't totally ignorant; he had heard of racquetball, but he'd never actually played. It was sort of like tennis, right? Did this constitute a real date or had George used the term loosely?

Dex's valet disappeared down the hall, and Ty tried to gather his composure. Would he be able to fake playing racquetball when he didn't even know the rules of the game, much less the object of it? Or should he fake an illness to get out of it?

"Dex, there you are." Bridget suddenly appeared at his door. "We need to hurry."

"We do?"

Impatience flared in her eyes. "Yes. Have you forgotten to look at your schedule again? Drake and Stern are meeting us at the racquetball courts."

"Who?"

"Drake and Stern."

"Do we have a business deal pending with them?"

Bridget narrowed her eyes. "You just closed a deal with them, Dex. What's wrong with you?"

"Oh, yes." Ty nodded, rubbing his head. "My mind's been foggy lately."

"Tell me about it. If I didn't know better, I'd think you switched places with someone else in Chicago."

He coughed, nearly choking with panic, and she paused and stared at him. He finally calmed himself; but he had to go along. "Right. Lead the way."

She folded her arms, drawing up the short tennis-skirt outfit a notch. "Aren't you forgetting something?"

He halted, searching his memory. He had on Dex's exercise shorts and tennis shoes; what else did he need?

She raised one dark eyebrow. "Your racquet and goggles?"

"Oh, yeah. Right." This woman made him feel about three years old and three inches tall. Flustered, he hurried back to the bedroom but couldn't find any kind of racquet amid the dozens of suits and ties in Dex's closet. He met her in the hallway. "I think I left it in the workout room."

George was waiting at the bottom of the stairs, Dex's gym bag and racquet in hand. "Here you go, Mr. Dex."

Ty took the gear but detected a slight quirky smile from George. "Thanks."

A few minutes later, he spent a harrowing ride in Bridget's silver Mustang convertible. It was her pride and joy, she'd told him, and came with all the latest bells and whistles, including seat warmers.

He much preferred Jessica's rattletrap, Nellie, and his old pickup truck at home. And he didn't need seat warmers in his car. He'd rather have a warm woman. A warm soft woman like Jessica. But that would never happen.

When they arrived, he and Bridget greeted the two businessmen. Apparently this outing was simply a goodwill game to smooth ruffled feathers over a recent takeover.

Ty's were definitely ruffled, though.

Thank goodness he wouldn't have to fake it through business talk, too. Under the guise of being polite, he insisted Bridget and Drake take the first court, and he watched, hoping to pick up the rules of the game. He had played baseball in high school, but this game was nothing like it. Bridget attacked the ball the same way she did the financial reports, with gusto and her cutthroat confidence, her lithe body sailing back and forth with ease, the short skirt accentuating long thin legs. Even half-naked, she held no appeal. What did Dex see in the woman? She was all sharp angles and planes, nothing like the soft curves and enticing femininity of Jessica Stovall.

Hell, he'd find a curvy, soft woman back home. One who liked the outdoors and didn't wear those stuffy suits.

Another court came available. Before he knew it, Ty was pounding the ball back and forth against the wall, dodging it as it zoomed back at him like a speeding bullet, the constant whip of the racquet contacting the ball zinging in his head.

"Dex, when did you start playing with your left hand?"

Ty froze, panicked and tried to hide his hand from Bridget. She and Drake had obviously finished their game. But he forgot to watch the ball. Seconds later, it smacked him in the head with the force of a jackhammer. He spun around, dropped his racquet and stumbled backward. Stars swirled in front of him just before his body collided with the floor.

JESSICA WOULD NOT ALLOW herself to act like a starstruck teenager. She had firmly put Dex Montgomery out of her mind.

Well, almost.

She steered Nellie toward the hospital. It would be easier if the nurses hadn't been talking about him last night when she'd made her nightly visit, raving about how he was not only the best-looking, most eligible doctor around, but that he had changed drastically in the past week, and he was now also the most generous.

She couldn't argue with either point.

Rumors had even started about naming the children's wing after him. How would Jessica ever forget the man then?

Disgusted with herself and this odd obsession with the *new* Dex Montgomery, she'd spent the morning out at the stables where she'd ridden and groomed her favorite horse, a gelding named Sundance. She'd thought the long ride in the fresh air and sunshine would clear her head, but no—she'd had silly fantasies about Dex riding up on a black stallion and sweeping her away into the sunset.

Fat chance of that.

She couldn't allow herself to get swept up in foolish fantasies.

Dex Montgomery struck her as a die-hard bachelor. And if he decided to change that status, a dozen women would be waiting in line to fill the bridal shoes. Women who could give him everything he'd ever want, from a blue-blood name that would suit the Montgomerys to prestige to...children.

Something she could never do.

Pushing aside the ache in her chest, she parked in her usual spot, then strolled into the hospital to check on Donny. A moment of fear gripped her when she saw his empty bed.

She caught the head nurse's arm. "Where's Donny?"

"Oh, hi, Dr. Stovall," Tina said with a smile. "He was doing so well we moved him into his own room."

Relief flooded her. "That's wonderful. I bet his mom is thrilled."

"She is. She started crying when Dr. Scranton gave her the good news."

"I'll go see them in a bit. I think I'll stop in and see Ashley first."

Tina nodded, and Jessica hurried to visit the three-year-old, worried Ashley might be alone or scared. Although a nurse or volunteer stayed with her around the clock, Jessica still felt as if she had to see her every day.

She'd even contemplated adopting her.

They all wanted to get Ashley through her surgery first, though, and see if her aunt came forward to take her. So far, she hadn't. In fact, her aunt already had seven kids and an impending bankruptcy situation. She hadn't even visited.

Jessica found the volunteer asleep in the chair beside Ashley's bed. Ashley lay snuggled up asleep, her injured leg bandaged from a recent infection.

Her heart breaking for the little girl, she nudged the woman. "You can take a break. I'll stay with her for a while."

"Thanks." The elderly woman smiled and stretched. "How long will you be here?"

*As long as Ashley needs me,* she wanted to say. But she bit her tongue, not wanting everyone to see how attached she'd grown to the child. "At least a couple of hours."

"All right. I'll be back by three. I could use some time to get my errands done."

Jessica gave her arm a squeeze and watched her leave. Pulling up a chair, she sat down beside Ashley and simply stared at the child's angelic face.

"Don't worry, baby," Jessica whispered, gently pulling the sheet up over Ashley's sleeping form. "I won't leave you alone."

She closed her eyes and imagined taking Ashley home, helping her learn to walk again, spending holidays and Christmases together. Thank God the precious little girl would receive the plastic surgery and wouldn't have to cope with such horrific scars—all because of Dex Montgomery.

It was too bad he wouldn't be a part of that happy little family scenario.

But she'd learned long ago not to count on miracles.

TY HAD NEVER been so humiliated in his life.

Well, except the time the bull had kicked him in the privates and he'd had to ice-pack his nether regions. But at least then he'd been home, and he'd hidden out in his bedroom. Sure, his brothers had ribbed him, but he hadn't had to face an army of paramedics, businessmen, the other people working out at the health club— many of whom were doctors and knew Dex— and a financial adviser who wanted to slice and dice him under a microscope. He had to face Jessica today as well.

Damn. He couldn't avoid her.

"You've got some goose egg," Stern said over the paramedic's shoulder.

"Are you dizzy?" the young emergency attendant asked.

"Dex, I still don't understand why you were playing left-handed," Bridget said. Her brittle voice grated on his nerves like a scrub brush against a saddle. But she just wouldn't forget that slipup.

He gave her a warning look, told the paramedic he was fine and pushed to his feet. "I'll be all right. It was stupid of me to look away. I know better."

The paramedic grinned. "Sir, you'd be surprised at the number of similar injuries we have. Golf is just as bad."

Ty did not feel better. And he prayed Bridget didn't have a golf date on his calendar. He'd probably knock himself out with one of those sticks; what did they call them—irons?

"I think we'll call it a morning," Stern said. Drake agreed. The two men shook his hand and left together. But Ty could have sworn he heard them snicker as they headed to the showers.

"I'll drive you home," Bridget said, taking his arm. "Unless you need to go to the hospital."

He did, but he didn't intend to tell Bridget he planned to see Jessica. He'd close the deal, then let things be done.

"If you experience dizziness or blurred vision, Dr. Montgomery—"

"He knows," Bridget said. "He's a doctor, remember?"

"Just doing our jobs," the paramedic said.

Ty thanked them, then headed to Bridget's Mustang for another crazy ride home. On the way, he'd have to engineer a reason why he was using his left hand to play racquetball when Dex was right-handed.

He suddenly had an idea. He'd convince her he'd used his left hand to give Stern the advantage. After all, she'd wanted them to mend ruffled feathers over M3I's takeover. He could insist that he was sacrificing himself for the job. It was a stretch, but maybe she would believe it.

He frowned, his conscience kicking in. One lie just led to another.

THE NURSES, AIDES and volunteers helped the children gather in the rec room for story time.

Little Ashley curled up in Jessica's lap sucking her thumb.

When Dex entered the room, the children whispered in excitement. They were accustomed to women nurses and volunteers, but having a man visit thrilled them even more.

Dex's gaze caught hers, and Jessica winced. She'd heard a rumor floating through the hospital that he had been hit by a ball, but she hadn't expected his entire forehead to show the damage.

"Oh, Dex," she whispered as he caught her gaze.

A blush crept up his dark jaw, and she couldn't help but smile. Good grief, even bruised and embarrassed, the man exuded more sex appeal than a movie star.

"You gots hurted?" one of the little boys said.

"Yep." Dex ran his fingers through his hair, pushing the locks back to reveal the full extent of the injury. A red knot the size of a walnut bulged outward, the skin already turning purple and yellow around it.

Ashley tugged at Jessica's lab coat and dropped her thumb from her mouth. "I gotted hurt, too."

Jessica laid her palm on Ashley's soft cheek. "I know you did, sweetie."

Dex stopped, smiled at Jessica, then knelt down to speak to Ashley. "Hey, princess."

"That's a whopper boo-boo."

Dex chuckled, a deep rumbling sound that made Jessica's stomach tighten.

"I know. Hurt like—" Jessica shot him a warning look "—heck. I should have kept my eye on the ball."

"I shud've stop and drop."

Jessica hugged her close. Since Ashley had been burned in the house fire that killed her parents, the nurses had talked to her about fire safety.

"We'll both know better next time, won't we?" Dex said with a wink.

Ashley nodded, her eyes big. "Dr. Jesse gots to kiss it and make it better." Ashley pointed to the bandage on her leg. "That's what she done fer me."

Jessica shifted, heat scalding her neck.

Dex grinned wickedly. "You know, I bet that *would* make it better."

"Maybe Dr. Jesse will do it later," Jessica said, aware the other nurses and kids were watching.

Ashley tugged on her arm again. "No, Dr. Jesse, now. He hurts."

Dex pushed his hair back again and leaned forward. "I think she's right, Dr. Jesse. It hurts real bad. Maybe you can take away the sting."

Jessica narrowed her eyes at him, promising retribution. But Ashley pushed at Jessica's arm and Dex's, so Jessica compromised by kissing her finger, then gently pressing it to his forehead.

TY READ THREE stories to the kids and helped the volunteers get them back to their rooms, then watched as Jessica tucked Ashley into bed and kissed her goodbye. His heart had completely melted. He wasn't Dex Montgomery, but for the moment, everyone thought he was, and he enjoyed helping them.

He was also beginning to really like Jessica. He'd have to remind Dex to be nice to her when he returned. But not *too* nice.

"I have an idea to raise money for the children's wing—"

"You've changed your mind about the donation?"

He heard the disappointment in her voice and briefly wondered if she might be playing up to him for the money. But he dismissed the thought immediately.

No, not Jessica. She was loving, kind, sincere. Honest.

Which he wasn't. Not since Chicago.

"I haven't changed my mind." He ached to touch her but refused to allow himself the privilege. "I don't go back on my word, Jessica. You can trust me. You'll get the funding."

Wariness flickered in her eyes, arousing his conscience. He wanted her to trust him, yet he was still lying to her.

But he couldn't tell her the truth yet.

Besides, it wouldn't matter. She was attracted to Dex. And he could never be his brother.

"Okay, Dex. What was your idea?"

"Let me take you to lunch, and we'll discuss it."

"I've already eaten."

"How about some coffee?"

"The hospital coffee is terrible."

"I saw one of those coffee places around the corner. They serve that fancy stuff with whipped cream and all."

Jessica finally relented. "Okay, I'd love a mocha."

Five minutes later, they'd walked to the Java Café. Ty ordered plain black coffee and was in heaven. Jessica gathered her café mocha and sat in a corner booth, torturing him as she licked whipped cream from the top with her tongue.

"Okay, tell me about this great idea."

"We'll put on a big backyard barbecue." He leaned back in the vinyl chair, feeling more relaxed than he had since he'd arrived in Atlanta. "We can invite investors to add to my donation, and we can also kick off the new playground project. It'll be like an old-fashioned barn raising."

Jessica's pink lips curled into a radiant smile. "That's a wonderful idea, Dex."

"And we can have games and pony rides for all the kids. Once people see those little innocent faces, they won't be able to write their checks fast enough."

Jessica sat up straighter, her excitement growing. "You're right. Oh, Dex, the kids will love it, too."

Ty grinned. "We'll have it on the Montgomery property."

Jessica laughed. "Are you sure that injury isn't affecting your brain? Somehow, I can't see your grandfather allowing a barbecue and pony rides at his house."

Ty bit the inside of his cheek. His grandfather might not go for it, but he would do his damnedest to convince him. After all, Ty had been doing everything he could do to fit into the Montgomery world. It was about time they loosened up around that house and learned something from the Coopers.

"Don't worry." He reached out and covered her hand with his, aware of the subtle tension between them. "I'll handle Grandfather. But this bruise is bothering me again. How about giving me another kiss to make it better? Maybe you could put a big lip-lock on me."

Jessica laughed again. "Good try, Doc. Next time you'd better be more careful."

He silently cursed himself for flirting with her; Gran always said he couldn't control his tongue around the women. He had to change the subject. "What made you go into medicine, Jessica?"

A second of silence stretched between them while she shifted in her chair and toyed with her coffee stirrer. "My mother, I guess."

"She wanted you to be a doctor?"

"No, not exactly."

"Come on, Jessica. If we're going to be friends, we can share a few dark secrets."

Jessica managed a smile. "It's not all that dark. It's just my mother… She was sick. Actually I was sick when I was little, too. I had severe asthma and had to be hospitalized several times."

"I'm sorry. That must have been tough."

Jessica shrugged. "It's scary being in the hospital when you're a kid. I guess that's why I went into pediatrics."

He sipped his coffee, watching her, admiring her more every minute. But the silences told him as much as her confession. She hadn't had a very happy childhood. "So what kind of illness did your mother have?"

"Alcoholism," she said, raising her face to gauge his reaction. "She pretty much smoked and drank herself to death."

Ty gritted his teeth. No wonder she hadn't had a happy life. "And you wound up taking care of her, right?"

She shrugged again. "She loved me, Dex. Don't get me wrong."

"But she wasn't much of a mother." It wasn't really a question, but a statement. Jessica didn't bother to reply.

She stared into her cup, stirred and drank another sip, a faraway look in her eyes. Ty wanted to reach out and hold her, take away that lingering sadness. But he couldn't start something that could never be. "I'm so sorry, Jessica."

She pasted on a smile. "I'm fine, Dex. I love my work, my house, my cat, my life. Now it's your turn. Tell me your dark secrets."

Ty stiffened. Here she'd bared her soul, told him things she rarely shared with anyone, and he looked nervous.

What could Dex Montgomery have to hide?

He'd grown up with money, education, connections. Did he have some sordid affairs he didn't want revealed? An ex-wife lurking in the past?

"I don't really have any secrets," Dex said. "You know about my family?"

"I know you live with your grandparents. What happened to your parents?"

She instantly regretted the question. The anguish in Dex's eyes was so genuine, she reached out and squeezed his hand this time.

"They died when I was three months old. I don't even remember them."

"Have your grandparents told you about them?"

A muscle ticked in his jaw. "Not a lot. There are pictures of my dad, of course, but they didn't approve of his marriage to my mother, so they've never talked about her."

"Oh, that's awful. Why didn't they approve of her?" Jessica asked softly.

He sighed, linked his fingers with hers, stared at their fingers. "She was a country girl, came from Montana. A rancher's daughter."

"That is a surprise." Jessica raised an eyebrow. "Do you know how they met?"

"No, just that they fell in love and married against the family's wishes."

"How romantic," Jessica said, wishing she could find true love like that. "But how tragic that they died and lost you."

That muscle ticked again. He downed the rest of his coffee. "Yes. Well, that's enough of that."

"I'm sorry if I upset you, Dex."

He shook his head, gathering his iron control. "It was a long time ago. Sometimes we have to put the past behind us, don't we?"

Jessica nodded. But obviously it came back to haunt Dex occasionally. Just as her past haunted her.

## Chapter Eleven

When Ty arrived home, he couldn't shake the conversation with Jessica. He'd told her they had to let the past go—but how could he do that when he didn't understand it? When it had affected him and Dex so, when it would affect their futures?

He found his grandfather in his study, sitting in his tall leather chair, holding his pipe, gazing out the floor-length window. He paused in the doorway and studied the older man's profile, recognizing the angular lines of his father's face in Grandfather Montgomery's chin and jaw. Had his dad and grandfather argued over Ty's mother? Was that the reason the Montgomerys had no pictures of his parents together? Had the Montgomerys signed Ty away the same way they did a business deal?

Had they thought about him at all the past thirty-two years?

"Dex?"

He jerked, realizing he'd been so troubled he hadn't noticed his grandfather turn in the chair.

"Did you need something, son?"

*Yes, some answers.* "I just came by to talk."

His grandfather's eyebrows rose in question. Ty bit his cheek to keep from revealing his thoughts. Instead, he inched inside the room. Dark paneling molded the walls from floor to ceiling, and the built-in shelves behind his grandfather held medical books and journals as well as books relating to business. But it was the pictures on the right side of his grandfather's desk that drew Ty's eye.

"Good God, son, what happened to you?"

Ty rubbed the knot on his head. "I was distracted, and a racquetball nailed me."

His grandfather stroked the long stem of the pipe. "You've seemed distracted since you returned from Chicago. Things didn't go as you planned?"

*That's an understatement.* "No, not quite like I'd thought. But I'm still hoping things will work out."

Ty indicated the photo of his father. "Dad's graduation day?"

Grandfather Montgomery's stern expression transformed into the first smile he'd seen on the man. "Yes, it was a proud day for all of us."

"He practiced here in Atlanta?" Ty asked, hungry for details about his father.

His grandfather nodded. "For a while. Your dad needed the medical background to run the company. I tried to get him to quit and return to his rightful position as chairman of the board. He refused." His grandfather's fingers worked the pipe. "Such a waste. Your father was a born leader. Intelligent, well-spoken, a real charmer, too, especially with the ladies." He leveled a look at Ty that spoke of sadness and love. "You're a lot like him, Dex."

Ty's throat closed. Maybe Dex was, but what about him—Ty Cooper, the other son?

God, how he wanted to ask.

"He was happy in practice?"

His grandfather nodded curtly, crossing one suit-clad leg over the other. "He claimed he was, but he lost sight of the Montgomery dream for a while."

"Because he had dreams of his own," Ty supplied.

"Because he was young and foolish, and he let a woman lead him astray."

Ty clenched his jaw. "You mean my mother?"

A hardness settled in his grandfather's eyes. "You have to understand, son. Your father was the namesake of the Montgomerys. He should have been loyal to his family."

"Maybe he needed something other than money and a big house."

Anger tightened his grandfather's jaw. "I only wanted what was best for him and the Montgomery family. And there were so many people, so many vultures ready to take whatever we had. They're still out there and you damn well know it." His grandfather stood and paced to the window. Ty saw him looking at a magnolia tree and wondered if it had any significance. "My father lost everything his father had built to a woman. I had to rebuild it all. And I swore my family would never do without the way we did when I was a child." He pounded his fist into his other hand for emphasis. "I built the Montgomery empire from scratch, and it was your father's turn to step in and take over."

"Only he married my mother, and he wanted to practice medicine instead of running the business."

The fading afternoon sunlight dappled soft rays over his grandfather's age-spotted skin, highlighting the tightness of his jaw. "I loved Charles, Jr. more than anything. I couldn't stand to lose him, but he chose to leave us behind instead of making sure that our family legacy continued."

Ty understood about family legacies. Could

he give up his family, the ranch, for a woman the way his father had given up what he had?

He didn't think so. He'd die without his land.

"But he loved my mother," Ty said, for the first time realizing the depth of that love. *And he wanted his legacy with his own sons.* So did Ty. Back at the Circle C.

"That marriage was a mistake. The Coopers wanted money from us the minute we met them." A vein bulged in his pale forehead. "We had to move here to Atlanta just to escape from them. I swear they probably convinced your mother to trick your father into marriage to get revenge on us."

Ty clenched his hands by his sides, ready to defend his mother. "What makes you say that?"

"I never wanted to tell you all this," his grandfather said, rubbing a hand along his jaw. "I know you want to think better of your own mother."

Ty *knew* better of her. She had to have loved his father. He and Dex had not been a product of some scheme of revenge born of the Coopers. He wouldn't allow himself to even think that. But neither could he argue their case right now. "I want to know the truth," he said instead.

"All right," his grandfather said reluctantly. "We lived in Rolling Bend, Montana, years ago. Your father and mother knew each other as kids."

"They did?"

"Yes, they were childhood friends." Charles Montgomery paused, inhaling the bowl of the pipe and settling the stem against his cheek. Ty realized he was smelling the remnants of tobacco and, for the first time in ages, longed for a cigarette himself. "You see, we ran the bank there in Rolling Bend, but the Coopers fell on hard times. We extended their loans as long as possible, but they wanted more and more. You know how people are."

Ty listened, thinking how proud the Coopers were, how difficult it must have been for them to beg for loan after loan.

"Finally I had to turn them down."

Ty guessed the rest. "They almost lost the ranch?"

"And blamed us." His grandfather frowned. "But I couldn't continue giving them money or we would have had to shut down." He paused, rubbing his pipe more vigorously. "We never saw eye to eye after that. Finally, we moved here to Atlanta and founded the medical conglomerate."

Ty's throat felt thick. "Did my mother and father remain friends?"

"No, they lost touch for a while." He cradled

the pipe in his palm. "But somehow they met up again. I think your mother came after Charles with the sole intent of convincing him to marry her so she could take him away from us."

Ty flinched. He couldn't believe that about his own mother or any of the Coopers. But his grandfather obviously did. And he'd done what he had to to protect his family.

"Maybe Dad decided that some things were more important than money," Ty finally said.

"You wouldn't say that if you'd grown up like I had." Grandfather Montgomery's voice rang strong. "And you don't seem to mind the pleasures it's given you over the years." His grandfather leaned back into his chair again, his face drawn. "You've done well for us, son. I'm proud of you. I know your father would be, too."

Ty stared at the tears in his grandfather's eyes and his chest constricted. Maybe his father would be proud of what Ty was doing with the family money. But he wouldn't be proud of the fact that his grandfather still blamed Ty's mother for taking him away. And he wouldn't like the fact that the boys had been separated. He knew that in his gut.

Ty had to figure out how to prove the Coopers' innocence to Grandfather Montgomery, though. And he also had a promise to keep to Jessica.

"Grandfather, I spoke with Jessica Stovall today. We're going ahead with the plans for the children's wing."

A long tense silence followed. "Bridget approved a budget?"

"No, not yet." Ty told him about the two accounts he'd found that they might be able to tap into.

"They're for emergencies, I imagine. But check with Bridget."

"I intend to." Exhausted, Ty rose, determined to study some more paperwork before dinner. Somehow, he would prove things to his grandfather.

"We are limited," his grandfather said. "You know that, Dex. We already have our projected figures for charities for the year. Don't lose your edge and screw up our profits."

Anger swelled inside Ty. His grandfather was resorting back to his tyrannical attitude—money first.

Ty paused. "I promised Jessica this thing would fly, and I intend to make it work. I'm also organizing a backyard barbecue as a fundraiser. We'll have food and pony rides—"

"Jesus, Dex, what's gotten into you? The next thing I know you'll be having a barn dance."

Ty grinned. "That's a good idea, Grandfather.

We'll add a barn dance as the grand finale for the evening."

"I—"

Ty held up a hand to stop his grandfather. "Like you said, Grandfather, I'm a lot like my father. And I think he would be proud of this idea."

Ignoring his grandfather's scathing look, Ty strode from the room, leaving his grandfather alone with his announcement and his memories of days gone by. Memories of the Coopers as vengeful people who'd stolen his son.

Now, he understood his grandfather's reasoning when he'd divided the boys. He'd probably decided having one boy was better than none. But why had they kept the boys from knowing about each other? From seeing each other?

Ty had to find some way to prove his grandfather had been wrong about the Coopers. And that Ty and Dex's mother had not been the sneaky villain Grandfather Montgomery believed her to be.

And when he accomplished that impossible feat, he still had to figure out a way to bring the two families together.

# Chapter Twelve

Once the idea of adopting Ashley took up residence in Jessica's mind, she couldn't evict it. Besides, occupying her thoughts and time with research into the proceedings had kept her too busy to dwell on the change in Dex Montgomery this past week and a half.

And the fact that she'd fantasized about making love to him last night.

Not only had Dex metamorphosed into a different person, but so had she—she'd lost her mind to her raging hormones. And if she didn't fight back, she would lose her heart as well.

She settled beneath a tree on the edge of the hospital property to sip some lemonade and watched Dex lead the crew in finishing the playground. She'd never imagined Dex had even held a hammer, let alone was able to use one deftly and orchestrate the work crew.

The plans for the barbecue had evolved more quickly than she could have dreamed, too. When

Dex Montgomery stepped up to take charge of something, he tossed the ball into play and kept it rolling. No wonder he had such a fine reputation as a businessman. When he made a deal, he followed through.

Unlike Jack, who had promised to love, honor and cherish her for better or worse, then had run when things got bad.

This morning, the kickoff event had begun with group efforts to build the therapeutic playground. Tomorrow the barbecue would end the weekend with a celebration of their accomplishments and the dedication of the funds. She couldn't believe the Montgomerys had agreed and had pulled it together so quickly.

Of course, money always talked.

That money separated her from Dex.

Her thoughts strayed to Ashley again as Jessica thought about the little girl's impending surgery, and her hopes for adoption.

So far, Jessica had spoken to the social worker in charge of Ashley's case, and she'd tried to push Ashley's aunt into making some kind of commitment, one way or the other. The woman still hadn't visited the little girl, and Jessica sympathized. The aunt had been struggling with other family problems for months.

That was the very reason Jessica had offered a sweet deal; the couple could have visitation rights and remain a part of Ashley's life if they chose. Jessica had no intentions of replacing Ashley's birth mother and father or blood family, and she promised to keep the memories of Ashley's parents alive, but she could fill the role of a loving mother and offer Ashley a good, stable life.

Now all she had to do was wait.

Wait and not get her hopes up too high.

She told herself she wouldn't, because even if the aunt took the child, Jessica could still visit.

Dex was a different story. They had no future together, so she needed to keep him at a distance. And that had proven harder every day during the past week and a half.

He bent to retrieve a board, and her gaze strayed to his backside. A pair of well-worn denim jeans hugged his muscular frame—she had had no idea Dex even owned a pair—and a T-shirt stretched across his broad shoulders, rippling muscles bulging as he lifted and worked with the wood. She fanned her face, burning up in spite of the pleasant spring weather. A drop of perspiration trickled down Dex's cheek, and he brushed it away with the back of his muscled arm. Jessica squirmed, a warmth stealing through her. She couldn't believe she was getting turned on watching the man doing manual work and sweating.

"He sure is a fine hunk of man," Tina, one of the nurses, said with a gleam in her eye. "I don't know what's keeping you from jumping his bones, Dr. Jesse."

Jessica laughed. "I don't want to be another number in his black book, Tina."

Tina clucked her teeth, settling chubby arms over her pregnant belly. "Honey, I know Dex Montgomery used to be a ladies' man, but he's been different lately."

Jessica couldn't argue with that.

"Maybe you should give him a chance. Life is too short to shut everyone out forever." She patted her belly. "I've seen the way he looks at you. Reminds me of the way my Toby looked at me when we first met."

Jessica bit down on her lip. Of course, he did look at her with lust in his eyes. But something more? No, Dex would only want a fling with her.

Wouldn't he?

TY WAS SO damn hot he needed a bathtub full of ice cubes to sit in to squelch his fever. The fever that had nothing to do with the temperature and everything to do with the fact that Jessica was staring at him with a hungry look that made him hard and achy. Of course, he hadn't been able to keep his eyes off her earlier when she'd jumped in to help with the building of the playground. She might be an educated doctor, but she was the least pretentious one he'd ever met.

Why couldn't he focus on the differences between the two of them instead of such similarities as the fact that they both liked kids and enjoyed helping others?

God, she looked damn enticing in a pair of jeans and a T-shirt. He could almost picture her on the Circle C, saddling up one of his geldings....

No. He couldn't.

Guilt pressed heavily into him. She thought he was Dex. Meaning she liked Dex Montgomery, entrepreneur, not Ty the rancher. For all he knew, she might hate horses.

Her gaze raked over his chest and down to his arms, and he clenched his jaw, slamming the hammer against the nail, forcing himself not to be too obvious. After all, the woman had avoided him for the past week and a half. It was probably for the best.

At first, he'd thought her schedule had simply interfered, but as the week had worn on, he'd realized she'd changed the time she dropped in at the hospital so they wouldn't bump into one another. She didn't want to see him.

At least she didn't *want* to want to see him. From the hungry look in her eyes, though, the attraction simmering between them was still there, maybe growing.

Rather, her attraction to Dex—the very reason he had allowed her to avoid him.

Soon, he and Dex would reveal themselves and return to their respective sides of the country. End of story.

His hands clenched around the hammer as thoughts of his two families interfered. Since his grandfather hadn't shown up to help with the playground, Ty had decided to use the time to think of a way to convince his grandfather to see the Cooper side of life. They were good, honest, hardworking people. So far he hadn't had any earth-shattering revelations.

His grandfather hadn't offered any more personal information, either. It was almost as if he'd regretted letting his guard slip that day, so he'd backtracked and acted as if the conversation hadn't happened.

His grandmother had been great, though. More affectionate and chatty than ever. And he was beginning to see why Dex considered George a friend. He did have a sly sense of humor about him.

Ty hammered a nail into the wooden board forming the customized jungle gym and smiled. Although Grandmother Montgomery had questioned the idea of a barbecue at first, George had shocked him by defending the suggestion. Finally convinced the barbecue would be fun, his grandmother had organized the event in two days. She'd even hired a band with a banjo player and had a stage set up for the evening show.

He hammered the last of the boards and checked to make certain the ends were smooth, thinking how much he missed his wood carving. Shrugging off the thought, he began to pack up supplies while the other volunteers did the same. Jessica approached each one, thanking them all as they left, and he paced himself so the two of them would be alone.

Minutes later, the sun pulled its last orange rays from the sky, dusk settled over the trees, and Jessica hurriedly gathered her things. She was getting ready to run like a jackrabbit with a fox on her tail.

Maybe it was the heat or the yearning he'd seen in her eyes all afternoon, but he couldn't let her leave without talking to her. Just the sound of her soft, sultry voice stirred his insides. At least he could take that memory back with him to Montana.

In spite of the guilt and warnings clamoring in his head, he found himself beside her, carrying her bag to the car.

"Thanks, Dex. You guys did a wonderful job.

The physical-therapy department will be impressed."

"My pleasure," Ty said, drawling out the word *my*.

Jessica's lips curled upward as she stuffed her things inside Nellie.

"How about dinner, Jessica?"

She hesitated, opened her car door and propped her foot on the ledge. "I...I can't, Dex. I promised I'd sit with Ashley tonight."

He reached over and tucked a strand of her soft hair behind her ear. The ponytail had fallen long ago and loose wavy tendrils had escaped, spiraling around her heart-shaped face. "You have to eat sometime. We can grab a quick bite somewhere. Finalize the plans for tomorrow."

Jessica's gaze darted to his chest, heat flaring between them. "I...I really can't, Dex."

He told himself not to push her, that it was better this way, but another voice inside him urged him to push harder. That Jessica was not a snobby doctor, that she might be able to accept the fact that he was a cowboy and that it wouldn't matter that he'd lied to her and concealed his identity.

Right. Just like Paula had balked at his way of life. And he hadn't even lied to her.

She slid into the car and turned the engine, and he realized he'd lost his chance.

The engine chugged but didn't turn over.

He leaned against the open car door. "That doesn't sound good."

She scowled and tried again. But the screeching sound continued.

"I think Nellie needs a new battery."

"I suppose," Jessica said warily.

"Why don't you let me drive you home. We'll get some dinner, pick up a battery, then I'll bring you back here to see Ashley."

She hesitated again, her gaze full of questions.

"Come on, Jessica." He brushed a gentle hand along her neck, then whispered in her ear, his traitorous tongue belying his good intentions. "Trust me. I won't do anything you don't want me to do."

A sigh escaped her, but she surprised him by looking into his eyes, holding out her hand and placing it in his.

*I won't do anything you don't want me to do.*

Dex's words rang in Jessica's head the entire way to her house. The problem was she wanted to do everything with Ty.

*Everything.*

Maybe Tina was right. She couldn't shut herself off from men forever. And Dex hadn't mentioned a serious relationship, so she didn't have to worry about marriage and the fact that he might want babies that she couldn't give him. He never had to know about her flaw.

He simply wanted to flirt. To have a fling.

Why couldn't she allow herself to enjoy what he offered?

She could, she told herself. She just had to be more modern in her thinking.

And she would.

No reason she had to go cold turkey from any physical relationship with a man; she was young, vibrant; she had needs. She would just keep her heart uninvolved. As she expected he would do.

No problem.

"Thanks for driving me, Dex," Jessica said as they parked in her driveway. "But I can call a service for my car."

Dex's warm hand covered hers. "No way. What kind of a gentleman would I be if I let you do that?"

Jessica laughed. "All right. If you don't mind, I'd like to take a quick shower before dinner."

"Fine." Dex's eyes twinkled with mischief as he followed her into the house. "If you need any help with your back, just holler."

Jessica laughed. "Make yourself at home, Dex. There's probably a beer in the refrigerator if you want a drink." Her pulse clamored as she headed to her bedroom, seriously considering his offer of help in the shower.

TY ITCHED TO follow Jessica into the bedroom and the shower, but he didn't move. He wasn't invited.

Damn, sometimes it was a pain to be a gentleman.

He liked Jessica, and that compounded even more guilt for lying to her. What would Gran tell him to do?

She'd tell him to leave Jessica alone.

In spite of that realization, he couldn't help but imagine stripping off his jeans and T-shirt and stepping beneath the spray of warm water with her. His body hardened. He could see the water droplets sluicing over her naked body, beading on her soft skin, cascading down her back, touching her in all the places he ached to touch.

He opened and closed his hands in frustration.

Exhaling and gathering his control, he went to the kitchen and grabbed a beer, hoping the cold liquid would douse the heat ripping through him. He was a gentleman, and gentlemen didn't lie or start relationships under false pretenses. She liked Dex.

Maybe when he returned, she'd want to be with him.

A sick feeling stole over him, but he pushed it away. His brother and she were more suited. Still…

He fought his feelings, wondering why he had so intense a reaction to her. He probably just didn't do enough socializing back in Rolling Bend. He knew most of the girls in town, so Jessica was just a change. That had to be it.

Trying to keep his mind off the bathroom, he studied Jessica's house. It was small, almost a cottage really, especially compared to the Montgomery estate. But it reminded him of the farmhouse at home, resurrecting the homesickness that attacked him daily. The den held a basket of sewing supplies, which surprised him, a needlepoint pillow she'd been working on lying on top. He thumbed through her stack of CDs, expecting to find jazz or rock, but found several country ones.

So, Jessica wasn't quite the person he'd pegged her to be at first. But the fact that she sewed and liked country music did not mean she'd like Ty Cooper or country life.

The kitchen had been painted a pale blue, and she'd hung yellow plates on the wall; the canisters were designed like Victorian cottages. Recipe books were stuffed haphazardly on the shelf above the stove, the stained pages a testament to the fact that she used them. He could picture her cooking in the small kitchen, making pasta or homemade bread or cookies, decorating cupcakes with a little girl or boy.

Trying to forget that image, he passed her white pine table and headed back to the den, but he noticed a second bedroom to the side. The walls had been freshly painted and a box sat by the door, drawing his eye. Curious, he peeked inside and noticed an assortment of baby paraphernalia. Baby blankets, stuffed toys, a Mother Goose book...

Had Jessica and her husband had children?

If so, why had she never mentioned a baby?

"What are you doing?"

Ty jerked his head up and saw her standing in the door wearing a fresh pair of jeans and a soft, pale green shirt that accentuated those gorgeous eyes. Her hair was still damp, and she'd left the ends loose so they lay in soft curls around her shoulders. Her face void of any makeup, he noticed a few freckles sprinkled across the bridge of her nose. She looked young and vulnerable and sexy as hell, and he wanted to kiss her and forget all the lies that lay between them.

But her gaze was riveted to the baby blanket peeking from the corner of the box. And when she lifted her face, a deep haunting sadness filled her eyes.

What in the world had happened to put it there?

# Chapter Thirteen

Jessica clutched the edge of the door, hating the fact that she couldn't hide her emotions. She should have gotten rid of the box of baby things long ago.

She would take them to the hospital soon and donate them to the children's wing.

"I'm sorry, Jessica. I didn't mean to pry."

"That's... I'm taking those things to the hospital," she said, her voice wavering only slightly even though the pain was choking her. Why was it so hard for her to talk about her loss? She knew she had to grieve and move on.

But she hadn't shared her feelings with anyone. No one could understand the devastation. The lonely, empty feeling she carried inside. The humiliation of having a man look at you as if you weren't a whole woman.

Dex reached for her, but she pulled away and headed to the safety of her living room. Seconds later, the scent of his cologne and then his powerful masculinity invaded her senses, and she felt him behind her.

A heartbeat later, his husky voice broke the quiet. "I wasn't snooping—I just... I don't know why I went in to the room."

She cleared her throat and faced him, blinking away tears. He obviously hadn't heard about her miscarriage. "Those are things I've collected to donate to the hospital."

"Then why are you upset?" He tipped her chin up with his thumb. "Jessica, sweetheart, tell me what's wrong."

The sound of the endearment stirred something inside her, breaking through the deep wall of pain. "Don't you know?"

He shook his head, his gaze dark. "No, but I'd like you to tell me."

The tenderness in his expression almost undid her. "I...I don't want to talk about it, Dex."

"All right." Dex's gaze flickered with disappointment. "Maybe one day you'll trust me enough to talk to me." He gestured toward the door. "Are you ready to go to dinner?"

Jessica nodded and led the way, his words echoing in her mind as they drove to the restaurant.

*TRUST ME,* HE'D SAID. But how could Jessica trust him when he was nothing but a liar? And if she did, wouldn't she be hurt worse when she discovered his deception?

Ty's hands gripped the wineglass, his chest constricting. The dinner had been nice; they'd eaten shrimp pasta at a small Italian restaurant and enjoyed the best wine he'd ever tasted.

But Jessica had been quiet the entire time.

"You must be tired from the day's work," Ty said, grimacing at his feeble attempt at conversation.

Jessica nodded. "I'll be over early to help with the picnic, though, and the games for the kids."

"They'll have fun." Ty tensed. Good grief, she worked herself to death, always taking care of the kids. He'd even heard she relieved some of the volunteers and came at night to sit with the children.

He hated to see her hurting and wished he could do something, anything, to ease whatever was tormenting her.

Not that he should expect Jessica to bare her soul. His secrets were enough to keep them apart. "You're not staying all night at the hospital, are you?"

Jessica shook her head. "No, but I promised Ashley I'd stop by."

He nodded and paid the bill. God, he wanted to kiss her and wipe away that sadness in her eyes. But he'd promised her he'd be a gentleman and that he wouldn't do anything she didn't want.

That meant not pushing her to talk until she was ready.

And not dragging her into his arms and kissing her unless he knew she wanted it. He thought he detected a hint of hunger in her eyes, but he wasn't sure.

They stopped at a small automotive shop, and he picked up a battery for Nellie, then he drove Jessica back to the hospital, the silence between them stretching taut with tension. As soon as they arrived, she jumped out of the car.

"Thanks, Dex. I appreciate dinner."

"I'll change the battery while you check on Ashley."

"You don't have to do that."

"I know, but I intend to, so go on and see Ashley."

She hesitated, then finally nodded, and he watched her go inside.

Dammit, he wanted to get her to open up to him. And he wanted to tell her the truth about himself so they could see if they could make a relationship work.

A real one—without any lies.

No, it wouldn't matter, he remembered foolishly. Her life was here. Not in Montana as a rancher's wife.

A HALF HOUR LATER, Jessica exited the hospital, her heart in her throat. She'd planned to stay longer, but Ashley's aunt had finally come to visit. Jessica had instantly felt like an outsider and had wanted to give them some time alone.

She should be happy for Ashley. And she *was* happy; Ashley would be with her real family. She would have brothers and sisters and a mother and father—a real family like Jessica had always wanted when she was a child. Yet when she'd seen Ashley's aunt there, for a moment, it had felt like losing her baby all over again.

Exhausted and dreading going home to an empty house, that nursery staring at her with such strained quiet, she didn't notice that Dex was sitting on top of Nellie until she almost ran into the front bumper.

"What are you still doing here?"

Dex raised a brow. "I wanted to make sure you got home okay."

Jessica sighed, hating the fact that she'd been curt with him when he'd been nothing but nice to her. The gentleman he'd promised to be. He'd even repaired her car.

He was really a much nicer man than Jack had ever been. She realized that now. Jack had been selfish from the beginning. Too controlling. Unemotional. And he'd never looked at her the way Dex did. Not with admiration and such potent desire that it rocked her common sense.

"I'm sorry. I guess I'm just tired."

"Ashley okay?"

She nodded. "Her aunt came to visit, so I didn't want to stay too long." She pasted on a smile. "And she needs her rest. Tomorrow will be a big day."

"The kids are excited, huh?"

Jessica squeezed his hand. "Yes, Dex, the nurses could hardly settle them down to sleep."

Dex chuckled. "I remember being that way before…on Christmas Eve."

Jessica frowned, remembering the lean holidays at her house.

"You don't have such good memories?"

His tender understanding was almost more than she could bear. She'd never been with anyone who could read into her soul the way Dex seemed to do. "Not many."

"Then you'll have to make some happy memories." He hesitated. "You can do things the way you want when you have your own family."

Tears welled in Jessica's eyes, tears she couldn't hold at bay. Especially after losing Ashley. Not that she'd ever had her.

"What's wrong, sweetheart?"

"I…I lost a baby," she said brokenly. "I… Last year. He would have been a year old now."

Dex's mouth tightened, but he didn't comment. Instead, he held out his arms. Jessica slid inside his embrace and let the tears fall. She'd finally found it in her heart to trust Dex, but she still couldn't tell him all her secrets.

And she wasn't sure she ever could.

Ty HATED THE PAIN in Jessica's voice, but at least she'd finally trusted him enough to confide in him. Not that trust did any good when she thought he was Dex.

He wished he could tell her everything about himself and this whole charade. Not that that would do any good, either. He would still go back to Montana and she would be here. But at least then he'd have a clean conscience.

But he couldn't reveal himself, not until he figured out a way to convince his grandfather that the Coopers weren't bad people. That his mother hadn't connived to steal his father from them.

Anger suddenly hit him. Jessica had mentioned that she'd divorced. Had her husband left her because she'd lost their baby?

JESSICA TRIED TO collect herself while she drove home. She hadn't meant to fall apart, but the day had been too much. And now Dex was following her home as if he was afraid she shouldn't be alone.

She didn't want to be alone tonight, she admitted silently. She had been alone for a very long time. But she knew better than to depend on anyone else.

With a weary sigh, she pulled into her driveway, cut the engine off and patted Nellie goodnight. Dex parked behind her and walked her to the porch.

"Are you going to be okay now, Jess?"

Jessica unlocked the door and turned to say good-night, knowing if she didn't, she would invite him in, and she would give herself to him, then she'd wake up in the morning and be alone.

She was too vulnerable tonight.

Maybe tomorrow when she was stronger she could have a fling, but not now, not with her feelings so fragile.

"Yes, thanks, Dex."

He traced a tender line around the outline of her face. "You don't have to thank me for caring."

Her throat closed.

"Jessica, will you answer me one question?"

She met his gaze, the stark turmoil blazing in his eyes a mirror of her own. "What?"

"Did your husband leave you because you lost the baby?"

His question stunned her, but not as much as the anger brimming in his words. But she couldn't go there tonight; she just couldn't. So she looked at him and lied.

"No. The marriage was on shaky ground before. We...we just weren't meant to be together." It was true, she realized. If what they'd felt for one another had been true love, they would have clung to each other in the face of their tragedy, not let it tear them apart.

He studied her for a long moment, then cupped her face in his big hands, angled his head and kissed her.

It was the tenderest, most gentle kiss Jessica had ever imagined, yet buried beneath that tenderness, the hot yearning of some primal need erupted between them. He sipped at her lips, then gently probed them apart with his tongue, tasting and teasing her with loving strokes that set her on fire. She answered with her own hunger, moaning as his arms enveloped her, clutching at his broad back and sinking into the pleasure of his touch.

Slowly, almost hesitantly he released her. "I told you I wouldn't do anything you didn't want."

Jessica nodded against his chest.

"Call me if you need me." With a whispered good-night, he released her, then walked back to his car, leaving her alone with her demons. She only wished she had the strength and courage to face them.

TY ACHED TO go back inside Jessica's home and make sure she was all right. Never had he wanted to protect a woman so badly in his life.

The irony of that thought didn't escape him. He wanted to protect her, yet if they carried things any further, he might hurt her. And she had the power to hurt him and didn't even know it.

Jesus, what a mess.

At least now he understood why the kids at the hospital meant so much to her. She hadn't been able to save her own baby, so she wanted to take care of the others. It all made sense.

And he admired her for it.

He steered Dex's Mercedes toward the office, the evening traffic thick, his mind spinning. The busy street noises bombarded him, reminding him he was completely out of place here. And that he could never truly be happy without the ranch, the wide-open spaces and big family. The smell of his grandmother's flowers around the front porch, the scent of the wood soap he used when he carved, the bustling energy of the kids at dinner and the clattering of pots and pans in the big old-fashioned kitchen, the pounding of Dodger's hooves on the path by the creek.

What about Jessica? What would she think of the Circle C? Would she like the rolling hills and lush greenery as much as he did? Or would the smell of cattle and the simplicity of ranch life put her off as it had Paula? Would she miss the fancy restaurants and shows and shopping malls?

Finally, he maneuvered his way into the parking lot of Dex's office complex and rode the elevator to his office. A light glowed from the inside, and when he opened the door, he was surprised to find Bridget in her office. Did she often work late on Saturday night? Was she working late because he'd asked for those monthly reports?

Regret pulled at him. The poor woman needed a life.

But they were alone in the office. If he went in, would she question him about his strange behavior? Or would she come on to him, thinking he was Dex?

Uncomfortable at the thought, he bypassed her office and hurried straight to his. A half hour later, he'd finished reviewing the funds and had pulled up the two accounts he had questions about. The company file told him zilch, so he searched the file cabinet for hard copies of old information. He had to find out what these were for in order to know if he could use the funds set aside in them. He headed to Bridget's office but decided to make copies of the files first to take home and review.

He slipped into the copy room and stared at the sophisticated machine. Seconds later, he punched a button, but a page jammed, and the machine spat papers everywhere. The documents sailed past him, flying to the floor so fast he couldn't catch them. Ty grabbed a couple that floated toward him, then dropped to his knees to catch another just as it jetted toward the underside of the machine.

A pair of purple high heels appeared in front of his face. "Dex, what are you doing?" She reached up, pressed a button, and the copier whirred to a stop.

"I…I guess I hit the wrong button."

"Obviously." Her bloodred manicured nails tapped along the metal top. "I don't understand why, though. You've used this copier a hundred times."

"It was an accident," he hedged, hurriedly gathering the papers.

Bridget knelt to retrieve one, picked it up and glanced at the contents. She swung an odd look his way, her expression a cross between irritation and…fear?

"What are you doing with these?"

"I wanted to ask you about these accounts— B & B," Ty said, standing. "They both hold sizable amounts of cash. Grandfather said they were probably some type of reserve account you'd set up for special funds."

Her gaze flitted sideways, her hand trembling slightly. She almost seemed nervous.

"They are," Bridget said in a curt tone. "I thought we discussed them last month."

Ty frowned. He had no idea if she and Dex had talked about them, and he had no way of knowing, barring calling Dex. Or giving himself away.

He had to play along.

"Right. Since they are on reserve, I'd like to use one of them for funding for the children's wing. That way we won't cut into profits."

"Let me take a look at them first. Then I'll let you know how much is available." Bridget smiled tightly. "That is if you're still going ahead with that project?"

Ty nodded. "I gave my word."

Bridget's stare turned icy. "Dr. Stovall just wants you for the money, Dex. You should know better by now."

Ty's fist almost crushed the papers in his hand. He wouldn't acknowledge her accusation with a reply. Instead, he simply turned and walked out. But he hated the tiny seed of doubt she had planted. He knew Jessica better, didn't he?

Was this doubt and mistrust the way of the Montgomerys? Was it the reason his grandfather could never bring himself to totally trust that Ty's mother had really loved his father? Had people used the Montgomerys so much that they couldn't take anyone at face value?

If so, he didn't like being a Montgomery.

And he wouldn't believe that Jessica was so devious. Jealousy had probably triggered Bridget's reaction.

Although her hand had trembled when she'd picked up the file. Had something else been wrong—had Bridget been nervous because he'd questioned her about those accounts?

## Chapter Fourteen

The next morning Jessica dressed in jeans and a denim shirt, stuffed her hair into a ponytail, then rushed to the hospital to help the staff with the children attending the barbecue. All the kids who were receiving ongoing treatment on an outpatient basis had been invited. The staff had commandeered a church bus to transport the children to the picnic. Dex's grandmother and volunteers had prepared goody bags full of crayons and paper and handheld games the kids could play with while recovering.

When the crew arrived after lunch, Jessica stared in shock at the transformation of the Montgomery property. They had set up the festivities on the grounds far away from the gardens and the pool area, deciding to avoid pool activities for the day. Decorations and balloons brightened the backyard. One area had been blocked off for games, another for pony rides, and a separate area near the pond held picnic tables draped in checkered tablecloths laden with foods, drinks and snacks. A clown roamed the growing crowd, telling jokes and making balloon animals for the kids.

The children squealed when they saw the ponies, their faces lighting up with smiles. Jessica wanted to hug Dex for giving them this special day. The volunteers guided the children who could walk toward the games, assisting others with the activities they could manage. Children gathered to play the balloon-toss game, to enjoy the sand-art tables, hula-hoop contests, bean bags, musical instruments, horseshoes and to have their faces painted. A separate booth full of volunteers accepted pledges and donations, also showcasing the plans for the hospital's future development.

Jessica searched the crowd and spotted Dex immediately. He was wearing a pair of faded jeans again, not designer ones as she would have expected, and a white shirt with the sleeves unbuttoned and rolled up, displaying his tanned, muscled arms. His handsome face took her breath away.

He stood beside an elderly man wearing a cowboy hat and brand-new jeans and a checked shirt. He'd tied a bandanna around his neck and wore a red apron. Dex leaned forward, obviously giving him tips on how to grill burgers. She was surprised he knew himself.

She'd never pictured Dex at a backyard barbecue but somehow the image fit and made him look even more appealing. In fact, he looked better in jeans than he did in a suit, like Clint Eastwood in an old Western classic.

"Here you go, sweetie." She wheeled Ashley's chair to a shade tree. "You can watch everything from right here."

"Dr. Jesse?"

Jessica stooped down to her level. "What, honey?"

"Can I wide de ponies?"

Jessica squeezed her hand. "Not today, sweetie. Your surgery is in a few days. The doctor said we can't take any chances."

Ashley's lower lip trembled. "But I wanna wide."

"I'll take you to pet the horses in a few minutes, I promise."

Ashley's eyes glittered with disappointment, but she perked up slightly. Jessica glanced at Dex and saw him watching her.

"I wike Mr. Dex," Ashley said.

Jessica silently dittoed the sentiment. In fact, she liked him too much. It was all she could do not to run and leap into his arms and kiss him.

Dex crossed the lawn to check on the games, but Jessica caught him. "Dex?"

"Yeah?"

She tucked a strand of hair behind her ear, suddenly nervous. "I just want you to know that I was wrong about you."

Dex narrowed his eyes.

"I used to think that you'd traded your medical degree for money. But I see now that you still use your talent to help people. And in a way you help a lot of people with the company."

A strange look tightened his face as if he didn't quite know what to say. She didn't give him a chance. She turned and ran back to Ashley.

TY HADN'T BEEN ABLE to take his eyes off Jessica, but he'd forced himself not to make a move yet. He didn't want to seem too anxious. After all, Dex was probably a pretty smooth ladies' man. Reality slammed into him.

If she was falling for anyone, it was Dex.

Not him.

"Are they done yet?" George indicated the charred burgers.

"Uh, yeah," Ty said. "You might want to move the others a little farther away from the flame."

"Oh, yes, right. Thank you, sir." George grinned,

looking pleased with himself that he'd mastered the art of cooking hamburgers on a grill.

Ty chuckled. He'd been shocked to see Dex's valet in starched jeans and a new cowboy hat, but he had to give George credit for trying.

"I'll check with you later." Ty started across the lawn toward Jessica, trying to tame his libido. This morning, he'd awakened from the most erotic dream. He'd been kissing her in a field of daisies, then they'd climbed on Dodger and ridden into the sunset like a couple in a TV movie.

Panic hit him. Why was he thinking like this? He'd never let a woman shake him up before, mess with his life, his responsibilities. How many times did he have to remind himself that when she discovered the truth, she might not even like the real Ty Cooper? Her earlier comment about Dex's work confirmed that she was attracted to the doctor. God, he hated to sound jealous of his own twin.

Still, did he dare trust that she might forgive the lies, that somehow the two of them, though from opposite worlds, might fit together? Pa Cooper had always said that it was the curse of the Cooper men—when they fell, they fell hard. It had happened that way with Chad when he'd met Jenny, and with Court and Brenda.

Was he falling hard for Jessica Stovall, a

woman he couldn't have? A woman who might be in love with his brother? Dammit. What a mess.

At least she was smiling this morning, that sadness in her eyes gone momentarily. His grandfather certainly hadn't been happy. He'd complained about how much time Dex had put into this project, about the expense of cleaning up after the ponies when the day ended. Ty had also noticed his grandfather and George arguing and wondered what it was about, but when he'd asked George, he'd mumbled something about airing dirty laundry that hadn't made sense.

"Hi, Dex."

Ty hesitated, wishing just once he could hear her say his real name. He stood within inches of her now, and it hurt not to touch her. But there were too many people around, especially children. And this day belonged to them. He even felt more like himself in his jeans and white shirt. Thankfully, he'd found a mall and had picked up some regular Levi's instead of having to wear those stiff designer ones in Dex's closet. He did hate using Dex's credit card, but he'd promised himself he'd pay him back.

"Hey, Mr. Dex."

"Hey, pumpkin." Ty bent over and pecked Ashley's cheek, sending her into a fit of giggles. "You having fun?"

She crossed her arms into an infamous three-year-old pout, reminding him of his niece, Angelica. "I wanna wide, but Dr. Jesse won't let me."

He cut a questioning look toward Jessica, but she shook her head, then tenderly brushed Ashley's bangs from her eyes. "I explained the doctor's orders, but I promised her we'd pet the ponies later."

Ty nodded. "Maybe we can compromise." He dropped to his hands and knees. "I'll be your pony today, Ms. Ashley. Dr. Jesse, will you help her mount?"

Ashley giggled and slapped her hand on the wheelchair. "Yes, Dr. Jesse, pwease."

Jessica laughed and scooped up the little girl, careful of her bandaged leg. "The horsey has to go slow," she warned. "And no bucking."

Ty made a neighing sound like a horse and dug his right hand into the ground as if his hoof was scratching the dirt. Ashley squealed. "You're sillwee, Mr. Dex."

Ty scratched the ground again, and Ashley laughed louder as Jessica settled her on top.

Ashley slapped Ty's side. "Giddy up, pony, giddy up."

Ty slowly gave the child her own kind of pony ride, his heart melting at the sound of her laughter. He felt like the biggest kind of fool when he saw his grandparents and George staring at him in shock, but the smile on Jessica's face made up for it.

Joey, the little boy he'd met at the hospital who was undergoing chemo, teetered up to his grandfather. The child offered the football to Grandfather Montgomery, obviously asking him to play, and Ty's gut clenched. Would his grandfather turn the little boy away?

To his amazement, though, his grandfather reluctantly accepted the ball and walked toward a clearing, then awkwardly tossed it to Joey. The boy returned it, his throw much harder than his grandfather's, and Grandfather Montgomery jogged to catch it. When he caught the football and spun around, Ty thought he actually saw his grandfather laugh. He wondered why he didn't do it more often.

JESSICA HAD NEVER LAUGHED so much in her life. The rest of the day flew by. She played games with the children and greeted the guests along with Dex to explain the plans for the new wing.

The donations had poured in.

When evening dawned, some of the younger children left for the hospital so they wouldn't overdo it, all of them pleased with their goody bags. A few others remained, along with a hundred or so guests. They gathered around a makeshift stage on the lawn where a country music band played tunes. Two of the board members cornered Dex, so Jessica sank into a chair to rest while the band warmed up.

Dex's grandmother slipped into a chair beside Jessica. "This was a great idea," Mrs. Montgomery said softly.

"I agree," Jessica said. "The kids had more fun than they've had in ages."

"It makes me happy to see their smiling faces."

"It was all your grandson's idea," Jessica added, wanting Dex to receive the credit. "He really threw himself into this project."

Mrs. Montgomery folded her age-spotted hands across her slender legs. "I know. I can't say when I've seen him so enthusiastic about anything." Her voice softened. "I was just thinking how much Dex reminds me of his father today. He looks just like him."

Jessica patted her hand. "I know you lost your son a long time ago, but you must still miss him."

"Terribly," Mrs. Montgomery admitted. "Charles, Jr. was our whole life. Especially since…" She sniffed, then dabbed at her eyes with a handkerchief.

"Especially since what, Mrs. Montgomery?"

The older woman dropped her hand. "Since

we couldn't have any more children." She paused and Jessica's heart squeezed, compassion budding in her chest.

"Oh, we tried," Mrs. Montgomery continued. "But I had two miscarriages after that, and Charles, Sr. got scared, so we gave up."

"I'm so sorry," Jessica said softly. "I know what it feels like to lose a baby."

"You lost a child?" Mrs. Montgomery's voice quivered.

Jessica nodded, a silent connection forming between her and the older woman. "Yes, last year." She cleared her throat, the burden of her secret lifting slightly. "Then I had to have surgery, so I can't ever have children."

Mrs. Montgomery's sympathetic gaze met Jessica's. "I'm so sorry, dear, and you're so young." She gestured toward the children gathering on the ground to hear the band. "But now I understand why you're so devoted to these children."

Jessica bit down on her lip, grateful to have someone who truly understood what she'd gone through. "I love them as if they were my own."

The two women sat in companionable silence as the band began to play a peppy country tune and people flocked to dance.

Mindy, a ten-year-old with leg braces, bounced up and down in her chair with the music. Dex noticed it at the same time as Jessica, walked over and bowed to the girl, holding out his hand.

Mindy pointed to her braces, but Dex simply shrugged, picked up the girl and planted her feet on top of his, obviously bracing her so she didn't have to put weight on her legs. Dex placed his hand on the young girl's back to support her. "Now, you settle those feet on top of mine, hold on, and I'll move us along."

Mindy obeyed, her pale face radiant as he danced them around the yard.

"I just can't believe how relaxed Dex has been all day," his grandmother said. "I've seen such a difference in him since he took that trip to Chicago."

"I know, so have I." He was a completely different man. Not that he'd ever been unkind or unlikable, just all business. He certainly had never noticed her. Jessica watched Dex dance Mindy around and swayed with the graceful sounds herself, knowing she couldn't fight it any longer.

She was in love with Dex.

She hadn't wanted to fall in love with him, but she could no longer deny her feelings.

What was she going to do about it?

TY HAD WATCHED Jessica with the children all day and had fallen more and more under her spell.

Yes, he had to admit he was fantasizing about taking her back to Montana. At least for a visit.

Which proved he was a first-class fool.

But for now, he'd have to be satisfied simply holding her in his arms, savoring the moment.

Because it would soon be over.

He stopped in front of her, bent and kissed his grandmother, then bowed to Jessica in a dramatic gesture, not surprised when she laughed.

"I don't know when I've ever seen two such beautiful ladies sitting side by side."

His grandmother blushed. "You are too much, Dexter. Those children are having the time of their lives." She squeezed his hand between her own. "You did a good thing here, son. I'm proud of you."

Emotions swelled in Ty's chest, robbing him of words.

"I can't help but wonder what we've been missing all these years…" she choked.

The sentence trailed off, and Ty wondered if she was thinking about pushing his father out of their lives, about not seeing Dex and him grow up together.

Then she patted Jessica's hand, and the moment was lost. "This lady deserves a lot of credit, too."

"That she does," Ty agreed. One of the little

girls waved at Ty, blushing when he blew her a kiss.

His grandmother laughed. "Why, son, you get more handsome and charming every day— you've got all the young ladies eating out of your hand."

All but the one he wanted, Ty thought, his gaze straying to Jessica. Though still wary, those grass-green gorgeous eyes sparkled with fun, with a teasing glint of sexuality and with affection.

"I've danced with all the other single ladies already." He gestured toward the young girls. "How about this one, Dr. Stovall?"

She laughed, obviously remembering the first time they'd met when she'd insisted on the title. "I suppose I could dance with the man who organized this wonderful affair."

He held out his hand, and she fell into his arms, her scent intoxicating. The band belted out "Georgia on My Mind" as Ty led her across the grounds, the scents of wildflowers, his grandmother's roses and Jessica's sweet scent floating around him. When he returned to Montana, would he be thinking about Georgia and the woman he'd left behind?

She traced a hand along his neck, then down to his collar and settled it on his shoulder. A shiver trembled through him.

"Dex, I can't tell you how much this day meant to the kids…and to me."

Ty thumbed her hair behind her ear, aching to kiss the tender spot. But there were still kids everywhere. "I know. But I don't want your gratitude, Jess."

Their gazes locked, and he saw the moment she understood his implication. He danced her underneath the shadows of a live oak, grateful the Spanish moss draping the leaves offered them privacy. Moonlight dappled her face, shimmering off her rich auburn hair. Darkness surrounded them, the house a shield from the other guests.

Her voice came out a husky whisper, matching the heat flaring in her eyes. "What do you want, Dex?"

He tried to forget the guilt nagging at him and pulled her closer, sucking in a sharp breath as her breasts pressed into his chest and her thighs brushed his legs. He framed her face with his hands, his breath hot, his voice an urgent whisper. "I want you, Sugar."

DEX'S HUSKY VOICE calling her Sugar sounded like music to her ears. Jessica wanted him desperately, but she could not make love to him with half the hospital staff, guests, children and his family nearby.

"Everyone's leaving," Dex said as if he'd read her mind.

A glance across the lawn told her he was right. So they wouldn't be rude if they left. Excitement skittered through her at the silent yearning in his eyes. But on the heels of desire rode fear. Could she really give herself to Dex and walk away afterward?

# *Chapter Fifteen*

The minute they stepped into Jessica's house, Ty's mouth found hers, covering her lips with his. Jessica threaded her fingers through his thick hair, her breath catching as he undid each of her buttons and opened the front clasp of her bra so her aching breasts spilled into his hands. His tongue and mouth were everywhere, dropping kisses down her neck, behind her ear, probing the sensitive skin of her cleavage. Jessica arched into him, her breath catching.

She wanted him, wanted him desperately. Just one time.

Sensations flooded her like fire as she gave in to the moment. With a low sigh, she threaded her hands through his hair and savored his kisses, his touches. He walked her backward, his knee parting her legs as they bumped into the sofa. But the sofa table shook and photos crashed to the floor, the only picture she'd kept of Jack landing beside them to stare up at her.

Jessica's stomach convulsed. She gripped Dex's hands, knowing she couldn't go through with this. She was not a one-night-stand kind of girl, and if she made love with Dex, she knew there was no going back. She was in love with him.

She had to break it off.

"Dex…" A tear rolled down her cheek in spite of her efforts to stop it. "Please, we have to stop."

He pulled away gently, cupping her face and looking into her eyes. "What's wrong?"

Jessica closed her eyes, battling tears and emotions she didn't want to share. "Nothing…. I just can't do this."

He didn't argue. Quietly, he dropped his hands, tenderly rebuttoned her blouse, then pushed himself up and sat down beside her on the sofa. When she would have jumped up and run away to the farthest side of the room, he clasped her hands and held them between both of his big hands, then placed them on his knee.

Jessica stared at their joined hands, her heart pounding, her chest aching.

"Talk to me, Jessica. Tell me what's wrong."

She struggled for courage to make the words come out. "I…I can't just sleep with someone, Dex. Not without a relationship. I…I'm sorry."

He clamped down on his lip with his teeth, his gaze dark. "Is that what you think I want?"

She saw hurt flicker in his eyes. "I don't know. But I have to be honest."

Emotions tightened his face, ones she didn't understand. "I like you, Jessica. I really do."

"I like you, too, Dex."

"And I don't want to hurt you." His voice sounded gruff. "I want you to believe that."

"I do." She squeezed his hand, her pulse racing. But he would anyway. Because he would want things she couldn't give him.

He saw the picture of the man on the floor, the cracked frame. Jessica snatched it up and stuffed it in a drawer in the end table.

"I don't know what he did to you, Jessica, but you have to let go of the hurt. Every man is not like your ex-husband."

A tear rolled down her cheek. "I know." Her voice was barely a whisper. "But it's so hard."

"I understand that, too." And he looked as if he did. As if he'd been hurt once upon a time, too. But she couldn't imagine anyone hurting Dexter Montgomery.

"But it wouldn't work, Dex," Jessica said quietly. "Remember your own rule about not mixing business with pleasure."

"Yeah, I remember." He raised his gaze to

meet hers as if he wanted to say more, his eyes stormy and tormented, but he didn't.

An ache filled her soul, threatening to tear her in two as she struggled not to fall into his warm embrace. His chest fell and rose with the steadiness of his breathing; hers trembled with every painful breath. Dex was a man to count on, a man who would never go back on his word, a man who always got what he went after. And he'd been nothing but honest with her.

If she told him her painful secret, he might say it didn't matter, a little voice inside her head whispered.

Jack had said the same thing in the beginning.

But he'd changed his mind later.

Dex might, too.

She couldn't bear to take a chance and spill her heart only to be hurt all over again.

GUILT PRESSED AGAINST Ty's chest as he watched Jessica fighting for composure, his body stirring at the sight of her lush curves and that vulnerable lip trembling. He hated the lies, the secrets, the pain in her eyes and the hurt he knew he would inflict when she found out he'd deceived her.

And he hated the fact that she might be in love with Dex. That he, Ty, had nothing to offer but himself and the ranch. No fancy life.

Jessica was right to have stopped them. He should have more control himself. He'd planned to, but when she'd looked at him with that naked longing, calm, practical Ty Cooper had lost all common sense. It had never happened to him before.

He'd carried the pain of Paula's rejection for years. He couldn't move forward in his life with anyone until he let go of that. And after meeting Jessica, he knew he wanted to move forward. But he would have to do it back in Montana, where he belonged.

Maybe it would be better if he left town and she never knew he had deceived her.

He brought her hand to his lips and kissed her fingers, one by one. "You're right, Jessica. Making love would have been a big mistake.

"I had a good time tonight." With one last glimpse of her precious face, he gave her a smile. "Just promise me that no matter what happens between us, you'll remember that kiss. And that I never wanted to hurt you."

She frowned, obviously puzzled at his statement. But she nodded, and he walked to the door. An oval mirror hung opposite the doorway, and he stared at himself in the mirror, not liking what he saw.

A man who had lied to a decent woman. A

man who had almost seduced her because of his own selfish needs.

He had always known who he was…at least back in Montana. But he didn't quite know the man looking back at him now. Impersonating a Montgomery had messed with his mind.

The old Ty never could have lied to a woman he'd wanted to take to his bed.

What had become of him? Had he become more like the Montgomerys? Some combination of the two?

All he knew was that he wanted Jessica.

He hated the fact that he had deceived her.

And he knew without a shadow of a doubt that he would have to return to the Circle C without her.

AN UNEASY FEELING clawed at Ty's gut the entire drive back home.

The Montgomery estate wasn't home, he thought, catching himself. He didn't take the time to ponder the slip, though; he was too worried about Jessica. And himself and this whole danged mess. It had been a mistake to come here, pure and simple. He didn't feel closer to his family—except for Grandmother Montgomery—and he was also confused about himself.

He'd never questioned himself or his actions before.

He didn't want to hurt Jessica. He wanted to protect her, to make her laugh, to see her happy.

He wanted to love her.

But he couldn't. He didn't have the right. And if he did, she'd end up hurting him when she discovered the truth.

He raked a hand through his hair, parked the car and hurried inside. Hell, he had to talk to Dex. They had to figure out a way to break the truth to the Montgomerys and to Jessica without making them hate them both.

The house was quiet as he entered. His grandfather must be in his office. Grandmother Montgomery might be out in the greenhouse, but he didn't want to face her right now, not with guilt pounding at him. He climbed the steps, not surprised George had turned down his bed for him.

But something else was sitting in the middle of his bed—a gold-embossed box.

Odd. Had George put it there? Or had his grandparents?

He walked to the bed, sat down and opened the box, his heart racing when he saw the contents.

Letters. Dozens of letters, handwritten in a woman's writing. He flipped the first letter over and emotions flooded him. They were letters his mother had written to his father years ago.

His hand trembled as he opened the first one and began to read.

Dear Charles,
It was so wonderful to see you again after all these years. All the memories of us playing together when we were children rushed back to me. I remember how upset I was the day you moved away. I ran out to that oak tree by the stream and cried for hours. Then I collected rocks and took them to your old house and threw them at the brick.

I wrote you letters every day, and it broke my heart when you never answered me. I thought you'd gone off and found some city girl and had forgotten me. I never dreamed that your parents hadn't given you my letters, or that you thought I had forgotten you.

Thank goodness all that is in the past now. I'm just so happy we finally found each other again. This time our relationship will last forever.

I love you, Charles. I always will. Maybe one day our parents will understand that and we can be together.
Love always, Tara

Ty's fist clenched the paper, perspiration trickling down his cheek as he laid it down and opened the next one. Another love letter. Several more followed, each filled with love and hopes that the family would one day understand how much Tara and Charles wanted to be together. The tenth one varied slightly.

Dear Charles,
I can't bear for us to be apart any longer. You asked if I would marry you, and you know I want to. I did so want your parents to approve, though, but I guess we both have to accept the fact that they're never going to want us to be together. Mom and Dad weren't too happy at first, either, but I think they realize how much I love you, and that it wasn't your fault your parents turned down their loan. When they get to know you better, they'll love you, just like I do. And when we have children someday, maybe they'll bring the family together.

I'm so proud of you for earning your medical degree and deciding to practice medicine. I know you're going to be a wonderful doctor.

Things have been tight here on the ranch for Mom and Dad. I had an idea to help bring the Circle C into the future. I've re-searched how cholesterol affects our health, and I thought that if we raise leaner meat, we might sell more. But you're the doctor, what do you think? It would take some re-search and we'd have to adjust our breed-ing, but in the long run it might be worth it.

Maybe we can talk about it next week when you come to Montana. I can't wait to see you again. Always know that my heart is with you.
Love always, Tara

Ty closed the letter, dropped his head forward and pinched the bridge of his nose to stifle the sting of tears.

Reading his mother's words brought her voice to life. He wished he could remember her, wished…so many things. And knowing how much his parents had loved each other meant everything to him. She'd thought grandchildren would bring the Coopers and the Montgomerys together. If only she'd known that it would tear them further apart. And that her boys would be split up, too.

Ironic. All this time he'd struggled for an an-swer to improve the Circle C when his mother had thought of it years ago. Only she'd died be-fore she had a chance to implement her ideas.

Ty placed the letters back inside the box and fastened the gold latch, a plan forming in his mind. He'd use the Montgomery knowledge and computers to do some research. Maybe he could make his mother's dream about the leaner beef come true. At least he could do that much for her.

But she'd wanted the Montgomerys to accept her. He'd heard the longing in her letters. And his father had obviously loved his mother or he wouldn't have kept all these letters. It would have destroyed both his parents to know he and Dex had been separated.

Could he make the second part of her dream come true, too? Could he convince the Montgomerys to accept her and the fact that she had really loved their son? Could he and Dex, her sons, finally bring the family together the way she had always wanted?

## *Chapter Sixteen*

Ty spent the next two days trying to iron out all the details of the hospital funding. And trying not to think about Jessica. She seemed to be avoiding him again, which was good.

Then why the hell did he feel so crummy?

He stomped up the steps after another lonely dinner and jerked off his tie, tossing it on the bed with a curse. He was just about to head to Dex's gym to work off his irritation when the phone rang.

He raced and picked it up, but Dex's voice sounded on the other end.

"Ty, it's Dex."

"Thank God it's you." Ty exhaled in relief. "I was afraid it would be someone I should recognize and couldn't. Doggone if this trading-places business isn't some flat-out nerve-rattling work."

"I know exactly how you feel."

"Is everything all right?" Ty asked, worry tightening his chest.

Dex gave him a quick rundown of how the family was doing, including the news about Chad and Jenny's pregnancy. Ty followed suit. "The Montgomerys are fine. I don't think they suspect, but George is a different story."

"Don't admit anything," Dex warned him. "George always played mind games to get the truth out of me when I was a teenager. If you give him an inch, he'll take a mile. He's relentless."

Silence stretched between them. Ty wondered if Dex missed the Montgomerys as much as he missed his family. And how could he explain Jessica?

"I think I've met someone," he finally said, solemnly.

"I thought you were going to keep Bridget busy with—"

"It's not Bridget. It's Dr. Jessica Stovall. The pediatrician."

"What about Leanne?" Dex demanded, a little more harshly than Ty would have expected.

"I told you," Ty said, "we're just friends. Leanne is like a sister to me. Nothing else."

"So, there has never been anything between the two of you?" Dex persisted.

"Never," Ty assured him. "Friends, that's all."

Silence stood between them for two long beats.

"Wait one cotton-picking minute," Ty said suddenly, suspicions dawning. "Are you and Leanne...?" He swore and pounded his fist on the dresser. "Don't even think about breaking that little girl's heart. Do you hear me, Dex. I won't have it."

"I didn't come here to break any hearts," Dex said tightly.

"Then what the hell's going on? Why all the questions about me and Leanne?" Ty snapped.

"It's nothing for you to be concerned about. I won't do anything I can't undo." Dex hesitated, his voice not very convincing.

"I'm counting on that," Ty told him bluntly. "This isn't about revenge of any sort."

"You're right," Dex said in a low voice. "It's about...understanding the past."

"Yeah," Ty agreed. "It's about the past."

"Call me if you need anything," Dex offered.

"We have to come clean soon. Now, tell me about these two accounts, B & B. Bridget said you'd discussed them."

Dex hesitated. "That's news to me."

Really? Maybe he'd misunderstood her. "Does she have power of attorney to write checks from them?"

"Not without my approval."

"You might want to look into it, then. I want to use one of them for funding for the children's wing, but she says she has to look them over first."

"I'll get right on it." Dex sighed. "Let's talk soon about making our big announcement."

"Right." Ty cleared his throat. "Soon." Just as soon as he explained the truth to Jessica. She had to know first. It would be better coming from him.

He hung up and phoned her immediately, hoping to ask her to meet him someplace private so he could talk to her.

But just like the other times he'd called today, she didn't answer.

JESSICA HAD BEEN SPENDING her mornings with patients, her lunchtimes with Ashley and her aunt, and the afternoons with more patients. After she finished with her last appointment of the day, she always returned to the hospital to help wherever she was needed.

Anything to avoid going home. And to avoid Dex.

She was afraid the next time she saw him she might lose her will to resist.

She'd timed it right and had missed him at lunch both the past two days. She also hadn't returned his phone calls.

She knew she was running scared, but there was no sense in torturing herself with fantasies about happily-ever-afters.

Not that Dex had promised anything or even mentioned the future.

Disturbed by that thought more than she'd imagined, Jessica decided she needed some fresh air and a visit at the stables with her horse, Sundance. Maybe the ride would clear her head and help her figure out how to end her personal relationship with Dex.

TY WAS WORRIED.

His stay in Atlanta was quickly coming to an end, and he didn't want to leave town without knowing Jessica was okay. He wanted to be sure that she and Dex could be friends and work together when his brother returned. After all, Dex wasn't on the ranch getting involved with some girl, leaving *him* in an awkward situation, was he? Nah, Dex likely thought with his head, not his heart, as Ty had always done.

He headed to the hospital to catch Jessica.

Of course, he'd been busy, and he knew she worked late hours, but couldn't she have at least *phoned* him? Was this what it would be like to be married to a doctor?

Had he actually thought about marriage?

He'd always thought he'd marry someday, but

to a hometown girl who liked ranching. Not to a woman like Jessica.

But an image of her flashed through his mind, and he could see her round with his child. Having kids wasn't all a picnic, but the good outweighed the bad, and it would be their baby, their little boy or girl to raise. He could teach him to play ball and to ride, build him a swing set, and she could teach him to be smart and…

Damn. He was getting ahead of himself. He had no future with Jessica Stovall. He was simply infatuated with her. He was confused about his life and his family, and she happened to be an enticing diversion. A pleasant, alluring diversion, but still a diversion.

That was all it was. It had to be.

But if she didn't hate him when she finally found out the truth, maybe he would invite her to the Circle C. See what she thought of the Coopers. Let her get to know the real Ty Cooper in his own element. Yeah, right, like she'd want to come to Montana.

He rubbed the back of his neck, exhausted just thinking about the deep hole he'd dug for himself.

At least he'd had one good thing happen— over the past three days he'd researched the cattle market, and he'd decided to go full steam ahead with his mother's idea about raising leaner beef. He'd already mapped out a plan. Of course, he still needed financial backing, but he'd work that out. Somehow.

Tonight, though, he had to see Jessica or he'd shrivel up and die from missing her.

The hospital loomed into sight, and his stomach jangled with nerves. He would not give in to his anxiety. Instead, he summoned his courage, parked, rushed in and rode the elevator to the children's floor.

He spotted Tina, Jessica's friend, as soon as he exited. Tina rubbed her stomach and smiled. "She's not here, Dr. Montgomery."

Ty sighed, frustration gnawing at him. "Do you know where she is? Did she go home?"

"Not home." Tina worried her bottom lip. "I don't know what's gotten into her. She's been obsessed with being here, so I told her to leave. She said she might go take a ride."

"In Nellie?" God, he hoped she didn't go too far. Nellie might not make it.

"No, to the stables. She keeps a gelding out there named Sundance." Tina grinned. "I think it's the only thing the woman does for herself."

Ty nodded. Jessica liked to ride? "Where is the stable?"

"It's called Crabapple Stables." She gave him directions and Ty took off. Gran Cooper believed in signs for everything—maybe Jessica's interest in horseback riding was a sign he and Jessica belonged together.

THE WIND FELT HEAVENLY on Jessica's face as she and Sundance crossed the grassy meadow and rode around the lake at the edge of the property. Wildflowers dotted the horizon, field lilies swayed in the breeze, and the scent of honeysuckle sweetened the air. She slowed Sundance to a walk and stopped beside the lake, dismounted, tied him loosely to a tree and let him drink while she found a seat beneath an ancient oak tree. Her mind had drifted a million miles away when the sound of hooves approaching jarred her from the peace of the lake. Not expecting any other riders to be out now since Gwen, the owner, was pregnant and due any second, she stared in shock as Dex crested the hill and rode toward her.

She had no idea he could ride.

Obviously, she'd never known the real Dex Montgomery. Since he'd returned from Chicago, it was almost as if he was a different man.

A nervous laugh escaped her; she was making too much of everything. There was no mystery behind Dex; she'd simply had preconceived ideas about him from business meetings and had never given him a chance to show his more caring side. She should have looked deeper.

His family had probably given him riding lessons when he was a kid while she'd traded lessons and saddle time for work, mucking stalls as a teenager.

What was he doing here? And what reason would she give for not returning his calls?

AN ODD PANG of homesickness settled in Ty's heart the moment he spotted Jessica. She looked so lost and vulnerable sitting beneath the shade of that tree, the sun fading behind her, the huge gelding standing lazily to the side. He could imagine her on the Circle C, the two of them taking an evening ride across Cooper land and, later, riding with their children.

God, he was starting to think crazy thoughts.

She started to stand as he approached, but he shook his head. "That's okay. I'll join you if you don't mind."

Her lip trembled, but she managed a weak smile. He tied Sylvester, the black gelding the owner of the stables had loaned him, beside her horse and patted his back, then turned to see her watching him.

His heart beat fiercely at the emotions swirling in those grass-green eyes. What was she thinking? Feeling?

"I've missed you. I called."

"I know," she said quietly.

He hesitated, his hands fisted by his sides so he wouldn't reach for her. "You didn't want to see me?"

She closed her eyes for a second, and his heart stopped.

"I'm sorry if I pushed too fast the other night—"

"It's not you, Dex." With a soft weary sigh, she finally looked at him again. "I…I was scared."

A battle warred within him. He knew she'd been married and divorced, that her ex-husband had hurt her. He didn't want to add any more sadness to her life.

"I'll make everything okay," he promised in a husky voice, although he had no idea how. "I realize you've been through a lot the last year. And I care—"

"Don't, Dex."

"Don't what?" He settled down beside her in a flash and took her hands in his, kissing her fingers, aching to hold her. "Don't tell you that I care about you? That I want to be with you, Jess?" Her chin trembled, and he lifted her face to his.

She gazed at him with such a mixture of fear and wariness, hunger and desire that he didn't know whether to love her or protect her from himself…

A shaky sigh escaped her. "Oh, Dex, I keep telling myself no, but…"

He should walk away. Instead, he tipped her chin up with his thumb. "But what, Jess?"

She placed her hands over his, her touch warm. "But I want you, too."

A slow smile spread on his face. A shy smile of surrender fell onto hers.

Knowing he *should* tell her the truth first, but hoping their lovemaking might bond them together, he ignored the warnings clamoring in his head. "You are so beautiful. I wanted you the minute I saw you in that boardroom."

"And I wanted you the minute I saw you in the airport."

Had she? Had she wanted him, Ty? Not Dex?

He squelched the thought, desperately wanting this moment, and lowered his mouth to hers, kissing her with all the pent-up emotions and fears he'd harbored the past three days without her. He was going to make love to her, then he would tell her the truth. It didn't matter if he was related to the Montgomerys, if he'd been wearing suits and pretending to be Dex—he was a Cooper at heart.

And Coopers went after the women they wanted.

His grandfather was right. When a Cooper man fell, he fell hard.

She sank into his arms, her hands clutching at him as if she shared his hunger. Still afraid she'd leave him when she learned the truth, but unable to resist this time with her, he reached for the buttons on her blouse.

Desperate for the feel of his skin, Jessica pulled at his shirt until he released her, yanked it off and threw it to the ground. The look he gave her screamed of hunger and desire and urgency—the urgency to brand her as his.

She had never seen such hot desire in a man before.

"Are you sure about this, Sugar?"

A slow smile lifted her mouth as she traced a circle around the hard bud of his nipple, then drew her finger down the center of his chest to his belt. "I'm sure. I can't help but want you, Dex."

His Adam's apple bobbed as he swallowed, the low growl he emitted part animal, the other part so male that her insides twisted with a deep ache that only he could fill. She tugged at his belt, watched his eyes darken as her hands brushed the bulge of his sex beneath his jeans, heard his breath hiss when she threw the belt on the ground and opened his pants. He allowed her the briefest of touches, her hand stroking his hard length before he pushed her hand away, shucked his clothes and stretched out naked above her.

"I want you naked, Sugar." With reverence, he slowly peeled away her clothes, the jeans, her socks, then inch by inch her panties, his tongue teasing each bare inch of flesh as he revealed it. She clutched the hard muscles of his arms until he rose above her and took her mouth again, this time hot and fast. His tongue tasted hers, probing and retreating, while his sex throbbed against her thighs.

He kissed a path down her throat again, loving each breast with his hungry mouth until she writhed beneath him. But he forced her to wait while he parted her legs and tasted her. Jessica moaned and pulled at his hands, but he settled himself at her heat and loved her until the tremors of passion rocked inside her.

Finally when she thought she'd die from desire, he rose above her, then looked into her eyes. His were hooded, dark with wanting, his breath a husky whisper against her trembling body as he plunged inside. Jessica dug her fingernails into his hard back and held on for the most passionate ride of her life.

TY PUSHED HIMSELF harder inside Jessica, her earlier words ringing in his ears.

*I wanted you the minute I saw you at the air-port. I've wanted you every minute since.*

She'd wanted *him,* not Dex.

And she was his now.

Forever.

No, he wouldn't allow himself to think that yet.

But he couldn't keep himself from having her, from making her his tonight.

He rained kisses along her jaw and ear, thrusting inside her, then braced himself on his hands and raised his upper body slightly. "Look at us, Jess. See how well we fit together."

Her gaze slowly traveled to the place where they were joined, her look of passion flaring deeper as he thrust in and out, filling her, retreating, then pushing farther inside her until there was nothing between them.

Nothing but hunger and need and sensations soaring out of control.

And the lies.

He silenced the nagging voice in his head, dragged her legs up around his waist and told himself they wouldn't matter, that the two of them were meant to be together, just as they were tightly bound together now. Then he pumped inside her fast and hard, pouring his heart into their lovemaking just as she cried out in sweet oblivion.

JESSICA COULDN'T BELIEVE she had made love to Dex, but emotions and passion and love had all mingled into one explosive moment.

They dressed quietly in the night air; her thoughts were jumbled. She needed to tell him now that it was over, that they couldn't continue to do this, but just as she opened her mouth to speak, the sound of horse's hooves jolted them.

"Dr. Stovall, come quick," Deanne, Gwen's twelve-year-old sister, shouted into the wind. "Gwennie's having her baby!"

"What?" Jessica ran toward her, Dex close on her heels.

"Hurry, she says it's coming now!"

Fear gripped Jessica—what if something went wrong? Although she'd been in the delivery room for several births and had done a rotation in gynecology when she was in med school, she was a pediatrician, not an ob-gyn. What if there were complications?

No. Dex was a doctor as well. Everything would be fine.

Only, she glanced sideways at Dex as the horses raced toward the stable, and his color had turned a sickly green.

PANIC SHOT THROUGH TY, his heart thundering in his chest.

Dear God, he couldn't deliver a baby—he wasn't even a real doctor.

Thank God Jessica was, though. She would take care of the woman.

They guided the horses to the edge of the stable, jumped off and handed them over to the stablehand.

"Come on!" Deanne yelled. "She's in the bedroom."

Ty followed Jessica at a dead run, pausing only long enough for her to grab her doctor's bag from Nellie. His stomach somersaulted when they opened the door and he heard the woman's moan.

"Go to her, Dex, and I'll call the ambulance."

Ty grabbed Jessica's hand. "No, you go. I'll call."

She hesitated, her green eyes narrowing. "What's wrong, Dex?"

"Nothing." He strove for a calm voice. "She knows you—she'll be more comfortable with you."

A loud scream punctuated the air, and Jessica nodded. Ty phoned the ambulance, his hands shaking so badly he almost dropped the handset before the call went through.

"What's the address here?" he asked the little girl.

She recited it, her eyes widening when another loud moan rumbled from the bedroom.

"It's all right," he told her as he hung up. "The ambulance will be here soon. We'll keep your sister comfortable until they arrive. Is there anyone else we need to call? The baby's father?"

"I already did," Deanne said. "He's on his way."

"Good girl."

She didn't look at all reassured. Her freckles danced across her wrinkled nose when she frowned.

"Why don't you go outside and watch for them," Ty suggested.

Grateful for something to do, the girl ran outside, letting the screen door slam behind her.

Ty took a deep breath and headed to the back room, the woman's moans tearing his stomach into knots. He had helped in problem births with cows and horses, but so far his experience didn't include two-legged creatures.

"Dex, hurry," Jessica called.

He rushed inside, reminding himself to remain calm. Jessica could handle this.

"How is she?"

"The contractions are two minutes apart. She's dilated nine centimeters." Jessica slipped into her professional mode, taking the woman's vitals and trying to calm her with a soothing voice. "Your vitals are good, Gwen. And the baby's heartbeat is strong."

"I feel like I need to push," the woman bellowed, her hips rising off the bed.

Ty backed away, feeling out of place.

"Dex, help me," Jessica ordered, quickly working to drape sheets over Gwen.

Ty froze.

"Dex?"

Shaking himself, he lunged forward and helped her lift the pregnant woman, feeling the first sense of connection when she gripped his hand and squeezed for all it was worth.

Sweat rolled down her pale cheeks as she gritted her teeth, breathing in and out with the pain.

"Don't worry, ma'am. We'll take care of things. Dr. Stovall here knows what she's doing." Unlike him.

Ty massaged Gwen's stomach while Jessica began breathing exercises. Tension gripped the woman's body. *Just pretend you're home helping one of the cows give birth,* Ty thought, and he said, "Just relax your right rear leg."

Gwen's eyes widened, a burst of laughter erupting.

"What did you say?" Jessica asked, her eyebrow arched.

"He said to…" Gwen clutched her stomach, laughing so hard her words broke. "To relax… my…right…rear…leg."

Ty stiffened, his gaze riveted to her foot as he realized she was right. He'd spoken to her as if he was helping one of the animals give birth! "I was...joking, trying to get her to relax—"

Gwen's laughter died abruptly. "It's coming!" She dug her fingernails into Ty's shirt. "Roger's going to miss it."

"Honey, I'm home!" a man called from the living room.

Gwen jerked Ty's shirt collar tighter, almost choking him. "Get that damn man in here now!"

Then everything happened at once. Jessica urged her to breathe, the baby's head crowned, Gwen's husband rushed in, the paramedics arrived, and Ty stepped back as Mother Nature took its course.

Seconds later, Jessica cradled the infant girl in her arms, cleaned her off, checked her over, then handed her to her mother. Goose bumps skated up Ty's neck. It was the most amazing thing he had ever witnessed.

"You were wonderful, Jess."

Tears misted her russet eyelashes. His heart ached for her. Was she thinking about the baby she had lost? "It's all right," he whispered, pulling her into his arms. "Everything's going to be fine, just trust me."

The baby let out a shrill cry, Roger rocked sideways, his face paling, and Ty and Jessica helped him lie down beside Gwen before he passed out. A few minutes later, when everything had calmed, Ty watched Jessica soothe the baby while the paramedics moved Gwen to the ambulance. He would never forget the moment the baby had come into the world. And the magnificent way Jessica had handled things. She was such a special woman, and for a moment by the lake she had been his. A knot tightened his stomach. Guilt followed. She deserved the truth. They couldn't make love again until he'd told her everything.

But he couldn't help but look at her with that baby in her arms and wish that it was his, one of the next Coopers to run the Circle C and keep up the legacy of their land. His breath caught, the memory of their lovemaking flashing through his mind. Dear God, he'd forgotten to use protection.

Maybe he'd be starting that legacy sooner than he thought. A smile floated on his face as he realized the idea wasn't nearly as frightening as he'd have imagined. But what if Jessica didn't want the baby?

What if she didn't want him or the Circle C?

JESSICA WAS A nervous wreck by the time Dex followed her home. She fumbled with the keys as she walked up her drive, trying to think of an excuse to send him home.

"Jess." Dex stopped behind her, took her keys and opened the door. "Can I come in?"

"I'm really tired, Dex. Can we call it a night?"

*Tell her, man, tell her now.* He hesitated, jamming one hand by the door. "I don't want tonight to be over."

"I just need to rest." Jessica gave him a pleading look. She did look exhausted. "Please?"

He studied her for a long moment but finally nodded, his eyes grave. "But first, I have something to say, Jessica."

What? She knew it had to end, but she wasn't ready to hear him say the words.

"I'm sorry. I forgot to use protection." He traced her cheekbone with his finger. "But I care about you, and I want you to know that if anything happens, we'll work it out together."

Oh, God, he meant a baby. He thought... He didn't know. Was he afraid? Now was her chance to tell him. She opened her mouth, but the words wouldn't come out. "It's okay, Dex. I'm on the pill," she said instead, her voice a mere quiver.

His gaze darkened. For a second, she thought disappointment flickered in his eyes. How would he feel if he knew the truth?

"I really have to go," she said in a pained whisper. "Good night, Dex."

He grabbed her before she could escape and

kissed her, a slow sweet kiss that brought tears to her eyes. "Good night, Jess."

She turned and ran inside and locked the door. Then she slid against the wall, wrapped her arms around her cat, sat down and cried.

## Chapter Seventeen

A bad feeling haunted Ty the next day, like the slow hiss of a snake at his heels. He had no idea why, but his stomach kept clenching and his nerves seemed to be out of sorts. It was almost as if he had a sixth sense that trouble was looming. He'd had the same feeling the day he'd ridden his first bull and broken his nose.

Adding to his anxiety, Bridget had acted strangely all morning, giving him odd, almost suspicious looks. She'd become irate when he told her he'd used the funds from one of those special accounts marked B & B and had accused him of squandering away the family money.

And he hadn't spoken with Jessica all day.

He chalked the bad feeling up to the fact that the day of reckoning had dawned. He had to tell Jessica the truth about his identity. He couldn't go on lying to her. He wanted to set things straight so they could move forward.

If there was any chance that could happen…

He would tell Jessica everything tonight.

Better to explain things than to wait until she found out some other way that might hurt her even more.

He drove to the restaurant where he was supposed to meet the board to hand over the fundraiser check, hoping to rush through the dinner and get her alone. On the way, he contemplated whether to take her in his arms and make love to her again before he confessed or wait and hope to use their lovemaking as a way to cement his apology.

JESSICA'S EMOTIONS RODE a rocky wave as she left the hospital and drove to the restaurant where the board had planned to honor Dex and celebrate the fundraiser's success.

When she arrived, she parked in the parking lot and sat in the comforting arms of Nellie for a few minutes, gathering her composure. After making love with Dex in the meadow, then delivering the baby with him, she had felt closer to him than she'd ever felt to another man.

And even more frightened.

She'd seen the excitement and awe in his eyes when he'd witnessed the baby make its entrance into the world, had felt the connection between them as they'd shared the birth process. When she'd first met Dex, she'd thought he didn't like children, but now she knew differently. After the paramedics had settled Gwen and the baby into the ambulance, there had been a blatant longing in his eyes. He wanted a family. Maybe even wanted the two of them to have a family together.

But it could never be.

Determined to get through the evening with dignity, she checked her lipstick, grabbed her purse and hurried inside. The Indian restaurant was one of Dex's favorites. The food was always spicy and the atmosphere charming. Most of the board members were already present when she entered the reserved room in back; the champagne was flowing and the mood was high.

She spoke to each of the board members, then greeted the Montgomerys.

"It's good to see you again, dear." Grandmother Montgomery squeezed her hand affectionately.

"Dr. Stovall," Grandfather Montgomery said with a firm handshake.

"Thank you for coming." Jessica's stomach fluttered when Dex entered. He looked impossibly handsome in a pin-striped Armani, his dark hair combed back neatly, his sexy grin in place. And the raw hunger in his gaze was directed at her.

A shudder coursed up her spine.

Maybe she should open up to Dex, trust him with her secret. Maybe he *really* wouldn't mind adoption....

"Hi, Grandmother, Grandfather, Jessica." He gave his grandmother a hug.

They chatted about the fundraiser and plans for the hospital, mingling with each of the board members before being seated and served dinner. Jessica tried to ignore the disapproving glare of Dex's financial adviser, Bridget. Dex claimed nothing was going on between them, and she believed him. Apparently Bridget wanted more, though. Would Dex give in to her?

No, Dex was not like Jack. She could trust him.

Not that it mattered. She and Dex had no future. Last night had proved that.

As they took their seats, Jessica's arm brushed Dex's, the hungry look he gave her a reminder of how she'd come apart in his arms the day before. How she could so easily do so all over again if she allowed herself the pleasure.

She dug into her appetizer and noticed Dex stare at the curried chicken, a small frown on his mouth as he tasted it. He grabbed his glass of water, chugging it.

"Whew, that was hot." He fanned his face.

Jessica laughed. "I thought you liked it spicy."

A sly grin pulled at his mouth as he leaned

over and whispered in her ear, "I do, but I'd rather have my women hot. Like you, Sugar."

Jessica blushed and rolled her eyes, on the verge of a wicked comeback when Dr. Epstein, one of the elderly board members, clinked his glass with his spoon, signaling everyone to be quiet.

His chair scraped the floor as he stood and held up his glass. "We're here to celebrate the success of the fundraiser Dr. Dex Montgomery organized, and to honor his generous contribution to the new children's wing."

Ty shifted, looking uncomfortable, and Jessica patted his arm. "Relax, Dex, you deserve all the credit."

"I'd like to make a toast." Dr. Epstein waited until the guests raised their glasses. "To Dex Montgomery—"

"Excuse me." Bridget suddenly jumped up and pointed to Dex. "That man is an impostor. He's not Dex Montgomery."

Ty GULPED AND DROPPED his fork, splattering sauce everywhere.

Both his grandparents turned startled looks his way, then glanced back to Bridget, the meal forgotten. Jessica cut her gaze toward him, her eyes narrowed in disbelief. And something else—hurt, as if the wheels were turning and she knew Bridget's declaration was true. Was she remembering all his little goof-ups?

He had to say something, to do something before Bridget ruined everything.

"Excuse me?" Frown lines creased Dr. Epstein's broad forehead.

Bridget flipped a thumb toward him. "He's not Dex Montgomery—"

"Bridget, can we go someplace private and talk?" Ty stood abruptly and moved toward her.

She slammed her hand on the table. "You aren't Dex, and I can prove it."

A wave of hushed whispers rippled through the room.

"This is an outrage," his grandmother said sternly.

"Young lady, sit down," his grandfather ordered.

"Not until you all listen." Bridget's voice rose. "I've noticed some odd things lately, like the fact that *Dex* messed up the copy machine, that he used his left hand to play racquetball instead of his right, that he didn't know if we had a deal pending with Drake and Stern when we had just celebrated closing it the day before he left for Chicago—"

"Stop it, Bridget. You don't know what you're doing." Ty gripped her arm, but she swung free and faced him, anger flaring in her brittle eyes.

Grandmother Montgomery paled, and Jessica sank back into her seat, her hand trembling as she pressed it to her cheek.

"I know exactly what I'm saying. I was suspicious all along. I'm exposing you as the fraud you are and saving the Montgomerys from a thief." Bridget suddenly waved a wallet in the air, turned and faced the tables of people. "I don't know what you're doing here and why you've been impersonating Dex, but I knew your signature looked different, and I have the proof right here—this insurance card."

Ty automatically reached in his pocket for his wallet, but it was gone. "How did you get my wallet?"

"I took it from your jacket back at the office when you were in the bathroom." She flipped out the card. "He might have Dex's driver's license, but this is his writing. He is Tyler Cooper from Rolling Bend, Montana."

"Oh, my God!" his grandmother cried.

Charles Montgomery flew out of his chair and grabbed the card. "Dear Jesus, it can't be."

Jessica knotted her hands. "Tyler Cooper? Who is Tyler Cooper?"

Ty's chest constricted at the disbelief and shock in Jessica's voice. "I…I can explain."

"It *is* you, isn't it?" His grandmother fluttered

one hand over her chest. "Oh, heavens, I should have known."

"You sneaky, lying impostor!" his grandfather shouted. "Did the Coopers send you here to steal part of the Montgomery fortune?"

"Who is Tyler Cooper?" Bridget demanded.

"Yes, what's going on?" one of the other board members asked.

"He's our other grandson," Mrs. Montgomery admitted softly. "Dex's twin."

"Twin?" Jessica rasped.

"What have you done with Dex?" Charles Montgomery asked.

Ty clutched the edge of the table as if his grandfather had slammed a fist into his chest. "I didn't do anything with him."

"Then where the hell is he?"

"He's at the Coopers'."

"I don't believe you." His grandfather jerked him by the collar. "Dex would never have gone along with something like this. How long have you been planning to come here—"

"Dex did agree." Ty gripped his grandfather's hand and pried his fingers loose. "And we didn't plan this. It just happened." He sucked in a harsh breath, remembering the hurt and betrayal he and Dex had felt when they'd first spotted each other. "We met at O'Hare Airport two weeks ago. You can imagine how shocked *we* were since Dex didn't even know he had a twin, and I thought my twin had died at birth. You and the Coopers lied to us all these years—"

"If he's Dex's twin, then these papers are null and void," Bridget cut in. "And so is the deal, gentlemen."

"What?" Dr. Epstein asked in a pained voice.

"No," the other board members gasped in worried voices.

"Dr. Stovall, what is the meaning of this?" Dr. Epstein asked in an accusatory tone.

Ty shook his head. "The deal is valid—"

"It most certainly is not," Charles Montgomery stated. "Not if you forged Dex's signature."

"That's right," Bridget said smugly. "Tyler Cooper has no power of attorney over the Montgomery finances."

"Charles, please…" His grandmother's voice quivered with tears. "Calm down. Let's talk—"

"There's nothing to talk about," Ty's grandfather stated baldly. "Not until I speak to Dex."

Ty backed away, hurt slamming into him. Was that what it had come down to? The way it had ended years ago? He was going to be thrust aside with no rights, no apologies, not only stripped of his heritage but of any financial rewards, just as they had done to his father.

Dex was the Montgomerys' grandson, not

Ty—he was a Cooper. And Coopers weren't good enough for the Montgomerys.

"Dr. Stovall, I can't believe you dragged the board into this mess," Dr. Epstein said in a low voice. "We'll see you at a disciplinary meeting."

"This isn't her fault," Ty said. "You can't blame her."

"She led the entire board to believe falsehoods," Dr. Epstein said. "So now it's between us, Mr. Cooper."

Ty turned to Jessica, praying she'd understand, that she'd see he and Dex had been victims in this whole ordeal. He had to make her believe he would fix things, that he would make things right. But the anger and hurt on her face only drove the knife deeper into his chest. He had lost complete trust in the only family he'd ever known, the Coopers, and now he was losing the tentative bond he'd built with his grandfather and grandmother Montgomery. He was losing Jessica, too. He could feel her withdrawing from him already.

With a pained sigh, she pushed her chair away from the table and ran from the room, destroying his hopes that she could ever forgive him.

JESSICA WRAPPED HER arms around her waist, the hurt so intense she felt it sucking the air from her lungs. Dex…no, this man named Tyler, a complete stranger…had lied to her. He had used her, slept with her, let her believe he cared for her…

She climbed into Nellie and dropped her head forward against the steering wheel, struggling to contain the tears.

Now she might lose her job, too. The hospital funding…dear God, they couldn't lose that money. She'd promised the children, the parents. Ashley was already scheduled for surgery the next day.…

The car door on the passenger side opened, and she clenched her hands around the steering wheel, knowing it was Dex…no, *Tyler*.

"Jessica, you have to listen, please—"

She raised her head and glared at him, shutting off his words. "Is it true?"

"I…" The agony in his face was intense, but she steeled herself against it. She couldn't feel sorry for this stranger, not after he'd deceived her. "Yes, I'm Ty Cooper. Dex's twin brother."

Hearing him actually admit to his lies sent a numbing pain through her.

On the heels of pain rode anger. She'd been such a fool. How had she not known? Bits and pieces of the past two weeks flashed through her mind like a trailer from a movie.

Dex…no, Ty walking past her at the airport as if he didn't recognize her. Disagreeing with his grandfather and agreeing to fund the children's wing. Helping to build the playground. Organizing the backyard barbecue. Riding a horse so well. Insisting she deliver the baby instead of jumping in to do it himself.

She'd thought he seemed like a totally different man after he'd returned from Chicago.

Because he was!

Good heavens, she'd been an idiot.

"Jessica, I never meant to hurt you." The deep husky resonance of his voice tore at her. "I promise you the funding for the center will go through."

"How can you say that?" she asked, her voice a pained whisper.

"Because I'll talk to Dex. I don't back down on my word—"

"Your *word?*" Jessica fought the urge to hit him. "You lied to me, you've been using me, and now you expect me to believe your word means something." She pressed a hand to her stomach. "I...I trusted you..."

He reached for her, but she backed away, battling the tears streaming down her face. "Jessica, please forgive me. I'll make it right. I swear I will. I may have let you think I was Dex, but I was hurting, too. I had to find out why our families had done this to us." He hesitated, panic tightening his voice. "All the things I said to you were true—the way I feel about you. I love you—"

"You don't know what love is," Jessica bit out. "You don't lie to the people you love."

"But I do love you," he said. "I want to marry you."

"Marry me?" Jessica hissed. "I don't even know you." She threw her hands in the air. "I thought you were Dex. And now I find out you're some stranger named Ty Cooper who lives in Montana."

Hurt momentarily darted across his features, but his voice was quiet when he spoke. "You do know me, Jess. Everything that happened between us was real." He pulled her hand into his, clutching it when she tried to pull away. "That was Ty Cooper at the board meeting who offered the money for the children's wing. *I* built the playground equipment and put on that barbecue. *I* made love to you."

Jessica wavered, the conviction in his voice even more confusing. "Jess, I do love you, and I want us to get married. I know you've never seen my ranch, and your home is here in Atlanta, but I really think you'll like the Circle C. We've got acres of land to farm and ride and a stream. The Coopers are all about family and building a legacy to keep the ranch. You'll love them, and they'll love you. And we'll take Sundance to the ranch, and we can take long rides at night together, sneak away to be alone."

She glared at him, the memory of the day before burning through her brain.

He continued, his arguments gaining momentum as if he really meant them. He patted the dashboard. "We'll even take Nellie with us. You can work at the local hospital there or open a practice if you want, and we can have kids. Lots of babies to love and take care of. My grandmother Cooper, she crochets an afghan for each new grandbaby. And our kids will love ranch life, with all the animals and ponies. And I do wood carving. I can make our kids a rocking pony and a cradle."

Jessica's heart squeezed, the pain like a knife twisting inside her. Oh, God, he wanted her and kids, and he'd even take Nellie.

"I have two brothers, and they're both married. One has a little girl named Angelica, who's a holy terror but we love her anyway, and my other one has twin boys."

"I have to go, De…Ty." She pulled her hand away, her ears ringing with his promises and the hope she heard in his words. His hopes for children, for a legacy. "I can't marry you."

"Jess—"

"No." She forced herself to meet his gaze. "I trusted you, and you made a fool out of me. I can never forgive that." She turned away, her jaw tight. "Besides," she said, knowing she had to say something to nail the coffin of their relationship shut, "I couldn't stand to leave the city and live on a ranch. The medical facilities wouldn't be up to par. Just let me know about the funding." Her voice almost broke, but she willed herself to remain cool. At least until she could get out of his sight. "Don't look so shocked. Dex would know that our relationship was all about business. Now, please get out of the car so I can leave."

The tension in the car seemed to go on for an eternity as he studied her, the light that she'd seen in his eyes when they'd been together flickering, then dying. Finally he opened the car door and climbed out. Jessica bit down on her lip, shifted Nellie into gear and drove away, forcing herself not to look back.

# Chapter Eighteen

Pain was crushing Ty's rib cage so tightly he felt as if his chest had sunk in. Had Jessica really meant what she'd said—that she couldn't live on a ranch? Had she only *slept* with him to secure the money for the center?

No, he couldn't believe that. That would mean he'd turned into a true cynical Montgomery, and Ty had too much Cooper blood in him to become so jaded. Besides, he knew Jessica... didn't he?

He drove toward the office, his throat thick with fear and regret and hurt. He really did love Jessica, he realized. It wasn't just an infatuation. He couldn't stand the thought of losing her.

He also couldn't stand the way his grandfather had looked at him. As if he was some low-down conniving thief.

Now he'd lost any chance of making friends with him.

Why couldn't his grandfather see that he had

never wanted the Montgomery money except to help Jessica?

But he'd ruined it all.

There was nothing left to do now but go home, lick his wounds and pray the Coopers didn't hold hard feelings about the twin switch. Maybe he could get to know Dex better.

He had to talk to Dex first, though, tell him what had happened and convince him to let the funding Ty had promised for the center go through. He swung by the office to pick up the files, knowing he had to have the details in hand to persuade Dex.

Then he'd go by the house, say goodbye to George, reassure Jessica the money would be provided for the center and head back to Montana.

A few minutes later, he stared at the computer screen in confusion. Apparently money had been lifted from the two B & B accounts several times over the past year. In fact, two checks for sizable amounts had been made out to Bridget recently. Did Bridget pay herself out of these accounts?

Dex had said he would look into it. He'd have to ask him when he talked to him.

The bad feeling he had that morning intensified when he heard Bridget's voice outside the hall, then his grandfather's. Their heated voices escalated, a door slammed, and he realized the two of them had gone into his grandfather's office for a closed consultation.

About him, he was sure. They were probably calling lawyers now, planning their strategy to legally bar him from the Montgomery fortune.

He should tell them not to bother. He didn't want their money and never had.

But he did want Jessica to have her funding.

His stomach moaned in protest just as the phone rang. He hoped it was Jessica, that she'd changed her mind and wanted to talk to him.

But his brother's familiar voice echoed over the line. "Ty, it's me, Dex."

Ty closed his eyes. Might as well find out how things were with the Coopers before he confessed he'd blown their cover. "Hey, what's going on there?"

"I'm afraid Pa Cooper had a heart attack."

Ty jerked his eyes open, his heart pounding. "How—"

"He's all right," Dex assured him. "We got him to the hospital, and he's in stable condition."

Ty felt dizzy. His grandfather was ill and needed him. The Coopers would all be there together, worried and scared, while he was here… "Are you sure—" he had to stop to clear his throat "—he's all right?"

Dex explained that he'd given him CPR and

that the attack had been mild, that he would need to rest for a while, that his grandmother had been strong, that all the family had gathered for support, even his niece and nephews. Anguish rolled inside Ty like a tidal wave. He wanted to be home with his family, comforting his grandmother and his brothers, reassuring Pa Cooper he would handle the ranch until he got back on his feet.

Dear God, what if his grandfather hadn't survived?

He had to fly home and make sure his grandfather Cooper didn't overdo it when he was released. Not that Dex wouldn't take care of him…

The full realization of what had happened hit him.

Thank God Dex had been there. That he'd been a doctor.

Ty stood. He had to leave as soon as possible. He had to thank his twin brother in person. To tell him that no matter what the Montgomerys thought, that even if they didn't want Ty, that Dex would have a place in the Cooper family. Forever. "I'll be on the next flight out."

"I figured you would." Dex paused. "But we need to straighten some things out first."

"I know. All hell broke out here today. I was getting ready to call you."

"What happened?"

Ty sighed. God, he was tired. "Bridget figured out I wasn't you. She announced it in front of the hospital board, including the Montgomerys."

"Damn."

"Grandfather Montgomery didn't take it well. He thinks I came here to steal his money." Ty gripped the phone with white knuckles. "And he wanted to know what I'd done with you."

Dex hissed. "Where is he now?"

"In a closed meeting with Bridget. They're probably trying to figure out how to protect themselves from me right now."

"I'll talk to him," Dex said. "And Bridget, too."

"There's something else we have to settle." Ty explained about the children's center, about how much the center meant to Jessica and told him about some of the children.

"We'll fund the center," Dex said without hesitation. "I don't care what Grandfather said, you're part Montgomery, just like I'm part Cooper. I'll make good on whatever you promised the hospital."

"Thanks, man." The weight of one boulder lifted from Ty's chest. Ty knew he was going to like his brother. Although they had lost valuable years, they would make up for lost time.

"Did I hear a hint of something personal between you and this Dr. Stovall?"

"Yeah, but nothing can come of it." He silently vowed to call the hospital as soon as he hung up and tell them if they wanted the money they couldn't fire Jessica.

"Sorry, man." Dex hesitated. "But listen, there's something else," Dex said in a low voice. "The company you met with in Chicago turned your proposal down. But I have an idea."

"I've already got a plan," Ty said. "In Mom's letters, she talked about raising leaner—"

"—beef," Dex finished. "We'll need more land—"

"—and I'll have to invest in different feed—"

"The Watley ranch will be perfect," Dex said. "We can lease the rest of the grazing land, and it'll benefit the Watleys."

Ty paused. Had Dex said *we?*

And they had been finishing each other's sentences. Was that a twin thing?

"You said we'll need more land. Are you planning to stay there?" Ty asked.

Dex hesitated this time. "Not permanently. But I'll provide the money."

"I don't want Montgomery money," Ty said tightly.

"Listen, Ty, I don't give a damn what my grandfather said. We're brothers, and if I want to be partners with you, that's my choice. The Coopers are my family, too."

Ty didn't know what to say.

"We can discuss it some more when you get here," Dex said. "Now, let me speak to Grandfather. Get him and Bridget in there and put him on speakerphone."

Ty buzzed his grandfather and waited, his stomach knotting when he walked in with Bridget.

"What the hell do you want?"

"Dex is on the phone."

"Dex! Is that you, son?"

"Yes," Dex finally replied, "I'm here."

"What the Sam Hill is going on there?" the old man demanded. "I don't know what kind of nonsense those people have put in your head, but I want you in Atlanta ASAP!"

"You have two options, Grandfather," Dex said, fury in his voice. "You may—"

"Dex," Bridget cut in sharply. "I cannot believe you're talking to your grandfather in such a manner. What has happened to you? Did you really agree to let this man pose as you?"

"Bridget—"

"Dex, darling," she purred. "How could you do this to us?"

"I haven't done anything yet," Dex said flatly.

"Please, Dex," Bridget hissed, "you must

admit this whole sham is incredibly bizarre. Perhaps you need—"

"Bridget," Dex interrupted smoothly. "I found the personal accounts you set up for yourself and the checks you wrote from those B & B accounts. You've been skimming large chunks of money for months, and we were too blind to see it."

"What…?" Bridget sputtered, her face paling.

"You can't deny it," Dex said. "I saw the figures. You're fired. Consider the money you stole your severance pay."

Ty barely contained a laugh at the stunned reaction on Bridget's face.

"This is all his fault." Bridget glared at Ty. "If he hadn't come here, we would have ended up together, Dex."

"Not on your life," Dex replied flatly. "Now get out."

Bridget stalked off, slamming the door behind her.

"I'm sorry, Dex. I—"

"Don't apologize, Ty. If you hadn't questioned those accounts, she might have taken money for years without us knowing it. Do you hear that, Grandfather? Ty saved us from being robbed."

"Only because he wants more for himself," his grandfather began. "I don't know what's gotten into you, son, but I'm warning you—"

"No, Grandfather," Dex objected. "I'm warn-ing *you*. On Saturday, if Pa Cooper is doing as well as expected, we're going to be having the mother of all barbecues at the Circle C."

"I'll be there," Ty said.

"By Saturday, if you're not back in Atlanta—"

Dex cut his grandfather off again. "If you want me back in your life, you will accept Ty and the rest of the Coopers as family. This ridic-ulous family feud has gone on long enough. It's all or nothing, Grandfather. No compromises... no negotiations."

"How dare you give me such an ultimatum!"

"If you're interested in remaining a part of my family," Dex informed him, "you'll be there on Saturday. Think about it this time.... How much are you willing to lose before you realize that life is too short?"

Dex didn't give his grandfather time to argue further; he disconnected.

Grandfather Montgomery glared at Ty, then strode out the door in a fury.

Ty's chest still ached. Love for the Coopers, fear for his grandfather Cooper, affection for his newfound brother and grandmother...hurt with his grandfather Montgomery. Anguish over losing Jessica.

It had been a stupid idea to come here. Grand-father Montgomery would never welcome him into the family or accept the fact that his mother had sincerely loved his father.

Just as Jessica would never believe that he really loved her.

He had to get home to see that Pa Cooper was okay for himself. Had to get home to the ranch where he belonged, where he could forget the pain of being rejected by the Montgomerys.

And Jessica.

He should never have let himself get involved with her.

Still, he reached for the phone to call the hospital and make sure she kept her job.


AFTER SHE'D LEFT Dex—no, Ty—Jessica had taken Sundance out for a long ride. She'd thought it would make her feel better, that the fresh air and time with the horse would free her mind.

It hadn't worked.

Instead, she'd worried about her job.

And she'd remembered last night, when Ty had joined her in the field, when they'd made love by the lake, when they'd delivered Gwen's baby. He'd been passionate and tender and loving.

She should have known then the man was an impostor.

But she'd been so wrapped up in the romance

and the passion that soared out of control every time she laid eyes on the man, she'd been oblivious to his lies.

Never again.

Brushing away more tears, she dragged the box of baby items out to her car. In the morning, she would take them to the hospital. Pausing by Nellie's trunk, she lifted the little yellow teddy bear and pressed it to her chest. Tears spilled past her lashes, the anguish of betrayal almost as sharp as the physical pain she'd felt when she'd lost her child. Ty's words tumbled through her mind, his vow of love even more agonizing than his deceit.

He'd claimed he wanted her to move to Montana with him. The smaller hospital wasn't important; she could work anywhere. But he wanted to have a family, raise babies…all the things she wanted but couldn't have. At least not in the normal way. He'd begged her to trust him, and she almost had, had almost told him her secret.

But he'd lied to her. How could she trust anything he said now?

And what if he told her he could accept the fact that she couldn't have children, then changed his mind later? She couldn't handle that pain again.

She glanced into the teddy bear's button eyes,

her heart squeezing. She'd give the little yellow bear to Ashley. She had to say goodbye to the past. To all her dreams and fantasies.

Just as she had to say goodbye to Dex Montgomery…no, to *Ty Cooper*.

Forever.

TY HADN'T SLEPT all night.

When he'd arrived at the Montgomerys', the house had been quiet. His grandfather and grandmother had gone out for the night. Even George had been suspiciously absent.

It had felt like a mausoleum, cold and empty, full of the ghost of his father and the way he had left the family. Just as Ty was now doing. Had his father felt this empty, sickening feeling that clawed at Ty's insides?

Ty stepped into the shower and grimaced. He hoped Dex could salvage his relationship with his grandparents. And George. He'd actually grown fond of the man.

He faintly wondered what George would think about ranch life.

Exhausted and physically aching from worry, he toweled off and went to dress. George had laid out the jeans and boots Ty had worn to the barbecue. He shouldn't have been surprised. The gesture spoke volumes. George obviously wanted him to leave just as his grandfather did.

Not wanting to prolong the goodbye, he dressed quickly, then hurried to the closet to retrieve his bag.

Instead, he stared at the suits and ties and designer shoes and realized that he had nothing here to take with him but the clothes on his back. He'd come here with Dex's suitcase and clothes.

This was Dex's home, Dex's family, not his.

And it never would be his.

He had been the foolish one to think things could have been different.

Other than the memory of his grandmother's embrace and the scent of her roses, there was nothing here he wanted to take with him, he realized as he left the room. Not the Montgomery money or their name. His grandfather hadn't been able to give him the thing he needed most: acceptance into the family.

Placing the Stetson he'd bought for the barbecue firmly on top of his head, he turned and strode down the stairs to say goodbye.

## Chapter Nineteen

Jessica pressed the teddy bear into Ashley's arms. "It's yours now, sweetie. For being such a brave little girl."

Ashley hugged the bear, her eyes already drooping from the sedative she'd been given to relax her before her operation. "Thanks, Dr. Jesse."

"You're welcome." Jessica gently brushed a kiss on Ashley's forehead. "Now when you wake up, your leg's going to be lots better. And soon you'll be running around like the other kids."

A smile tugged at Ashley's lips. "Sing hush baby."

Ashley's aunt Carlotta began to hum "Hush Little Baby," and Jessica joined in, the little girl fading into sleep just as they finished. Jessica and Carlotta tiptoed to the corner of the room to wait for the nurses to wheel her to surgery.

"Thank you for taking such good care of my

niece," Carlotta said, a tear seeping from her dark lashes. "And for understanding why it took us so long to decide about taking Ashley in."

"How are things?" Jessica asked softly.

Carlotta folded callused hands over her arms. "Better. The insurance company finally came through, so I think we're going to be all right."

"Good. Let me know if I can help you in any way."

Carlotta nodded. "You look sad today, Dr. Jesse."

Jessica smiled. Unfortunately this morning her concealer hadn't done its job covering the dark circles beneath her puffy eyes. "I'm fine, just tired. I'm so glad Ashley will have her family around her. Family is everything."

She sighed as the nurses slipped in to wheel Ashley to surgery, then excused herself. She needed to help plan the going-home party for Donny. The children here were her family now. At least for a little while, until the disciplinary committee met.

She tried not to think of Ty.

TY FOUND HIS grandmother having breakfast by herself in the garden. Tension tightened his shoulders as he approached her. She glanced up, a dainty teacup in hand. Her expression reflected a hint of wariness, but a small smile lined her slender face. "Good morning, Ty."

He tipped his hat, then removed it and laid it against his chest.

She gestured toward a wrought-iron chair. "Will you have coffee with me this morning?"

He nodded, his heart in his throat as he watched her thin hands pour from the silver coffee server on the table. "I…I'm not sure what to say except I'm sorry."

She closed an age-spotted hand over his. "No, Ty, you aren't the one who needs to apologize or explain things. We are."

Ty stared at their joined hands and felt a connection he didn't want to lose. "I didn't come here to hurt anyone. Or to take money from the Montgomerys."

Compassion and regret flickered in her eyes. "I know that, son. Even though we never got to spend any time with you as you grew up, I've thought about you every day." She smiled, her eyes glittering with unshed tears. "I used to wonder what it would be like to see you and Dex together. Every Christmas, every birthday…" Her voice broke, and Ty squeezed her hand.

"How…how did it happen?" Ty asked gruffly.

She set her teacup down, the china clattering. "We were all hurting back then, the Coopers, your grandfather and I. It was such an awful time." She dabbed a lace handkerchief to her eyelids. "You see, your father fell in love with your mother when they were just children."

"I know. I read some of Mom's letters. I heard about the bank loan, the move. That they met and fell in love again when they were older."

She nodded, fidgeting with her handkerchief. "But your grandfather Montgomery forced your father to choose between Tara and us."

Ty nodded this time.

"You have to know why, though. I realize Charles comes across as cold and hard, but there's more to him than that. He's been a wonderful husband and provider. And sometimes when people act angrily, they're really afraid, but they don't want to show it." She hesitated, her words measured. "You see, Charles grew up in such hard times. He never wanted his children to suffer."

"He caused my father to suffer."

"I know." She sniffed, a tear rolling down her cheek. "But he regretted never making up with your father. All that stubborn pride."

A few shaky breaths filtered through the painful silence.

"We wanted a large family," she went on to explain. "But after Charles, Jr., I had several miscarriages." She shrugged, but he saw the old pain lingering. "Each time, your grandfather became that much more protective of Charles. He was our only child, and he didn't want to lose him."

Ty waited, watched her struggle. He didn't want to understand now or feel anything for his grandfather, but he did.

"When Charles, Jr. talked about marrying Tara, your grandfather was afraid he might lose his son for good, so he gave him an ultimatum."

Ty shook his head. So stupid. "But his plan backfired."

His grandmother nodded sadly. "Yes, and when he lost your father, I thought your grandfather would wither and die. He...he became even more obsessed with work and making money. He grew hard."

Ty's chest ached.

"Then Charles and Tara died..." Her voice broke. "We were all devastated. And you boys were left, and the Coopers wanted both of you. He was afraid they would win. And frankly so was I." She folded the handkerchief into a triangle. "The Coopers felt the same way. You see, we wanted both of you, too."

Ty swallowed, fisting his hands together. It must have been an impossible situation for all of them. But so unnecessary.

His grandmother cleared her throat. "The court finally ruled that each of us would take one of you. The judge stipulated that we had to agree that neither of you ever found out about the other." With frail fingers, she lifted a long silver chain to a locket nestled inside her blouse. She popped it open and gestured toward the pictures inside. A picture of Ty on one side, Dex on the other.

"I love you, Ty." Emitting a shaky sigh, she pulled him into a hug. Ty closed his arms around her, glad he had come here, if for no other reason than to know that this grandmother loved him.

And that at one time Grandfather Montgomery had loved him as well.

JESSICA KEPT HER morning appointments at her practice, then rushed to the hospital to help with the plans for Donny's celebration. His heart surgery had been a major success, and he was finally going home today.

Ashley had made it through surgery fine and was resting in recovery. Breathing a sigh of relief for both the children's sakes, she wove her way into the children's wing, then to the rec room where the nurse's aides had begun setting up for the party.

All morning, gossip had flown through the halls about the debacle with Dex Montgomery at the board-meeting celebration.

She felt like a fool in a million different ways.

Tina loped in, carrying decorations. She beamed a smile at Jessica. "It's a good day for the children."

Jessica nodded and grabbed the paper plates just as they slid from Tina's hand. "We have a lot to be thankful for."

The balloons bobbed as Tina placed an anchor on the string and put them in the center of the table. "I heard about Dr. Montgomery's twin. What's his name?"

"Ty Cooper," Jessica said through clenched teeth.

"Whew-ee." Tina wiggled her eyebrows. "He sure did look like his brother."

"Yeah, he fooled us all," Jessica muttered.

Jessica set out the party cups while Tina situated the cake and other treats on the table.

"That he did," Tina added. "But he did some good things while he was here. After all, he got us the money for the children's wing, he volunteered with the children, helped build that playground."

"Uh-huh."

"And the man did have a fine set of pecs."

Jessica rolled her eyes. "You're a happily married woman, Tina."

"But not blind." Tina chuckled. "Is it true what they're saying?"

Exasperated, Jessica threw one hand on her hip, deciding she might as well come clean. "What are they saying?"

"That he never knew his brother. That they met in an airport and were shocked to find each other." Tina's voice grew low. "That the Montgomerys forbade their parents to get married, and when the boys' mama and daddy died, the grandparents divided them up and never told each other anything about the other one."

A knot gathered in Jessica's stomach. "Yes, it's true."

"You know twins are supposed to have a special bond." Tina *tsk*ed. "Bet those boys felt that void all those years."

Jessica winced. She had heard the pain in Ty's voice when he'd relayed the story and when he'd told her about his parents' deaths, but she'd been suffering too much herself to really think about Ty and Dex's situation. Or to feel for them. "I imagine so."

"And they traded places so they could meet the grandparents they'd never known."

Jessica nodded. "But they lied to everyone."

"Yeah, that wasn't right. And maybe they hurt people when they did it." Tina made a clicking sound with her teeth. "Then again, if I'd been in their shoes, I don't know what I would have done."

Jessica caught Tina's gaze and saw the sparkle of understanding in her eyes. She wanted a family so badly. If she suddenly discovered she had a sister or brother or even grandparents somewhere, wouldn't she do anything she had to do in order to be with them?

"I THOUGHT YOU'D be gone by now."

Ty pulled away from his grandmother's hug, bracing himself against his grandfather's angry voice. "I'm on my way out the door."

His grandfather's hooded gaze took in Ty's hat and boots.

Grandmother Montgomery tugged on his hand. "You are going to talk to that nice Dr. Stovall before you leave, aren't you?"

Ty hesitated. "If she'll talk to me."

"Why wouldn't she?" Grandfather Montgomery barked. "She got what she wanted, some of the Montgomery money."

Anger burned Ty's throat. "Jessica Stovall is not the one obsessed with money, Grandfather. She's the most generous, kindhearted woman I've ever known, and I won't let you slander her. I called Dr. Epstein, too, and made sure she isn't blamed for this, that she keeps her job, so you'd better not interfere."

A vein bulged in his grandfather's forehead. "Don't take that tone with me, young man."

Ty met his grandfather's hard gaze, his own filled with fury. "It seems to me that you put your trust in the wrong hands. Bridget was the one skimming money right from under your nose." He brushed his grandfather's shoulder as he stalked past. "Yet you don't trust Jessica just like you didn't trust my mother."

"She wanted revenge—"

"Charles," his grandmother warned.

"She loved my father, *your* son," Ty said, going nose to nose with his grandfather. "But you were too afraid you'd lose him so you pushed him away. If you don't believe me, read the letters she wrote my dad. He kept them all." Ty stalked to the door. "They're in my…Dex's room…that is, if you have the courage to learn the truth and to admit you made a mistake." He sighed in disgust. "My mother had hoped that if they had children, that the grandchildren would bring the Coopers and Montgomerys together."

Squaring his shoulders, he strode to the door without looking back.

To his surprise, George was waiting in the foyer, looking uncomfortable himself. "Thank you, George, for everything you did. Especially for showing me the letters."

George nodded, the corner of his mouth twitching with a smile. "And thank you, Mr.

Ty. You were good for this house." George's eyes misted. "I do hope we see you again."

Ty shook the man's hand. "If there's ever anything I can do for you…" Ty let the sentence trail off when his throat tightened.

George looked sheepish. "Well, I wouldn't mind an authentic pair of those chaps."

Ty grinned, relieved at George's sense of humor. "I'll see what I can do." He started to shake his hand, but George hugged him instead.

"Take care, Mr. Ty."

Ty nodded, then walked outside and climbed into the taxi he'd called earlier. As the cab pulled away, he took one last look at the Montgomery estate, memorizing it in his mind. Like a black hole, an emptiness swelled inside him. He didn't expect ever to see the place again.

Or the family within it.

# *Chapter Twenty*

Jessica saw Ty enter the party, and her heart lurched into her throat. Dressed in jeans and that denim shirt, he looked like the cowboy she now knew him to be.

Damn him.

The mere sight of his handsome face made her knees buckle.

But a relationship couldn't be based on lies or a lack of trust. And they had both those in caboodles.

Including her own painful secret.

She finished serving the cake and watched him weave through the kids, talking to each one of them.

"Hey, partner." He high-fived Joey, the little boy who was undergoing chemotherapy, the one who always carried the football.

"Hey, Dr. Dex."

"Actually, it's Mr. Ty," Ty said with a grin. "I'm Dex's brother."

"Wow, you look just alike."

Jessica wiped her hands on a napkin and approached the circle. "Yes, Mr. Ty was playing a joke on all of us, making us think he was his brother."

"What's it like to be a twin?" a redheaded little girl asked.

"I really don't know," Ty said. "It's a long story, but I just found my brother."

Ty's gaze cut toward Jessica, but Ashley waved to him before he could speak to her. "Sing today?"

Ty nodded and Tina produced a guitar.

"He's been doing sing-alongs when he's visited," Tina informed Jessica, something Jessica had barely seen because she'd avoided him so much.

If only she'd avoided him the entire time, she thought dismally, she wouldn't have a broken heart.

Ty strummed the chords, his husky baritone rumbling out "She'll Be Coming 'Round the Mountain." The children joined in, singing and clapping, and Jessica relaxed, momentarily letting her guard slip. Even if Ty had fooled them all, at least he had done good things for the kids. She only hoped his brother didn't undo the good when he returned.

Tina leaned against Jessica's chair. "He's something else, isn't he?"

Jessica blinked back tears as he laid the guitar aside, then nodded.

Ty removed his Stetson and settled it on Joey's slick head. "Wanna keep this till your hair grows back, bud?"

"Wow, cool! Can I?"

"Sure. I've got another one back at the ranch in Montana." Ty folded his arms, cocked his head to the side and grinned. "It looks better on you anyway."

Joey whooped, his thin face glowing with pleasure. Jessica hugged her arms around her middle as the rest of the kids hugged him and said goodbye.

Finally he approached her. "Can we talk?"

She hesitated.

"Please, Jess."

Tina nudged her toward him. Not wanting to make a scene in front of the kids, Jessica followed him into the hallway, the children's voices echoing behind them.

"I talked to Dex, and the money is all settled—he agreed to keep the funding for the children's wing intact."

A small knot of worry evaporated from Jessica's chest. "Thank you."

"Glad to do it. I talked to Dr. Epstein, too. Your job is safe, Jessica."

A long silence dawned between them, filled with tension.

"I'd like to stay and talk, but I have to catch a plane." Ty shifted, jamming his hands into the pockets of his jeans. "My pa Cooper had a heart attack."

Jessica's breath caught. "Oh, Ty, I'm so sorry. Is he—"

"Dex says he's okay, but I need to be there. The family and all…"

"Of course. I'm sure they miss you."

Ty shrugged. "There'll be some explaining to do."

He looked so lost, those dark eyes gazing at her hungrily, begging for understanding, filled with worry and such confusion that Jessica ached to reach out and touch him, to comfort him and tell him what he wanted to hear.

His confession of love still echoed in her mind.

But she couldn't give him all those babies he wanted. And in spite of the fact that he'd lied about his identity, deep down she knew Ty Cooper was a good man. A man of his word. A keeper.

Only, she had to let him go.

So, she said nothing.

"Jess, I'd like to talk to you later—"

"There's nothing else to say, Ty. I hope your grandfather is okay." Thrusting up her chin, she turned and walked away, forcing herself not to look back or to think about the pain she'd seen in his eyes. She should have been grateful he'd managed to help her keep her job.

Instead, it was a silent victory. Because for once in her life, she wanted something even more than she wanted her work.

She wanted Ty.

TY'S PLANE WASN'T DUE to leave for three hours, but he saw no need to stick around the hospital or to return to the Montgomerys, so he took a cab to Hartsfield Airport, remembering the last time he'd been there—when Jessica had picked him up in Nellie.

He'd come to Atlanta hoping to reconcile his past and his two divided families, but he was leaving with a trampled heart and a family more divided than ever.

He should feel good that he'd tried, but a deep sense of failure weighed on him. Like the dreamer Gran called him, he'd wanted everything to work out.

Suddenly a horn blared and a dark Cadillac cut the cabdriver off. The cabbie cursed and swerved, barely avoiding a fire hydrant, then squealed to an abrupt stop with the front wheels on the curb.

"What the hell?"

He turned in shock to see George helping his grandmother Montgomery from the Cadillac.

"Oh, no, these crazy people are going to rob us!" the cabbie muttered in broken English.

"It's all right," Ty said. "I know these people." His grandmother's diamonds glittered in the sunlight as she waved a frail hand. "Can you wait a minute?"

The driver pointed to the escalating numbers. "It'll cost you."

"No problem," his grandmother bellowed. "Just hold on."

Anxiety knotted his chest as he climbed out and faced George and his grandmother. Something must have happened for them to run him off the road. "What's wrong?"

A sheepish grin tugged at George's face. "Sir, your grandmother needed to speak with you."

Ty's eyebrows shot up. "Did something happen to Grandfather? Have you heard from the Coopers?" God, no, had Pa Cooper's condition worsened? Was he too late?

"Relax, son." Grandmother Montgomery laid a gentle hand on his arm. "Everyone's fine. But there's something I have to tell you before you go."

"What is it, Grandmother?"

"Your grandfather was wrong about that nice Jessica Stovall. I spent some time with her at the barbecue, and she's a fine young woman."

Ty chewed the inside of his cheek. "Yes, she is."

"She's a special lady you've got there."

"She's not my lady."

"What are you going to do about it?"

He swallowed. "About what?"

"About the two of you." She clucked her teeth. "I saw the way she looked at you that day at the barbecue, and I saw the way you looked at her."

"It's over, Grandmother."

George's smile faded. "But, sir—"

"I asked her to marry me," Ty blurted. "But she refused. The idea of ranch life didn't appeal to her."

"Nonsense," his grandmother whispered. "That girl is in love with you. She's just upset right now."

"You love her, don't you, Mr. Ty?" George asked.

"It doesn't matter," Ty said, heat climbing his neck.

George made that infuriating *tsk*ing sound. "Of course it does, sir."

His grandmother took his face between her hands, her eyes gazing into his. "Yes, it does matter. I was wrong in not supporting your father when he wanted to marry Tara. I won't stand by and let you make the same mistake by leaving the woman you were meant to be with behind. Especially if you're leaving her because Charles made you suspicious of her."

Ty's heart flip-flopped. "I appreciate that, Grandmother, but I told you, Jessica—"

"—loves you," his grandmother said with conviction.

"No, she might love Dex, but not Ty Cooper, the rancher."

"She loves you, Ty. I've seen her around Dex, and trust me, there was nothing there." His grandmother grinned. "Sure, she's mad and hurt that you deceived her, but love only comes along once in a lifetime. Don't throw it away."

"I'm not. I told you she refused my proposal."

His grandmother worried her bottom lip with her fingers. "Tell me what you said to her."

Ty reiterated his proposal as best he could remember. "She loves kids, and I promised her we'd have a dozen and she could work at the local hospital."

"Oh, dear."

"What?"

His grandmother frowned. "Oh, dear me."

Ty threw up his hands, totally baffled. "What did I do wrong?"

The cabdriver honked, but George wagged

a finger at him. "Just hold your horses, mister. We have a crisis!"

Grandmother Montgomery laced both hands around his. "Ty, there's something you should know. Jessica lost a baby—"

"She told me that," he said softly.

"But she didn't tell you the rest, did she?" His grandmother paused, her voice a pained whisper. "That she can't have children at all."

Ty's throat closed. "What?"

His grandmother nodded, a sadness darkening her eyes. "It's true. She was devastated. I heard it in her voice."

And her husband left her because of it, Ty realized, nausea rolling in his stomach. And Ty had been so eager to make up to her for lying, to propose, he'd ranted about having a family legacy, about having babies and how his Gran Cooper made each one an afghan. And earlier, he'd told her he'd take care of things if she was pregnant. He'd hoped she was.

"Oh, God." He dropped his head forward, knowing he must have hurt her terribly, that he'd added salt to the wounds he'd already inflicted and to the ones she'd suffered from her first marriage. No wonder she didn't want to talk to him. "I really screwed up."

His grandmother pressed her forehead against his, once again cradling his face in her hands.

"I understand the fact that she can't have children hurts, but if you love her enough, son, you can work it out."

It did hurt to know she couldn't have children, that they could never have a baby of their own, yet there were other ways...

Ty's gaze met hers, hers full of wisdom and love.

George nodded his agreement. "I say, go get 'em, cowboy."

Ty suddenly smiled. He had no idea how he would fix things, but he was damn well going to try. After all, a man's woman was more important than his horse.

And he'd die for his horse.

JESSICA PATTED SUNDANCE'S flanks, kicked her heels and breathed in the fresh country air as she rode across the pasture toward the pond. Tears stung her cheeks with the breeze, the sunlight fading over the horizon casting murky shadows over the land, the darkness mirroring her own gray mood.

Ty was probably on a plane now, headed back to Montana. Back to his family and his life. Maybe he'd find another woman to share it with.

She fought against the jealousy that thought evoked, a little voice inside her head whispering that he deserved someone else. Someone who wasn't a coward.

She had been furious with him for lying to her.

Yet hadn't she lied to him?

She'd been so caught up in her own pain that she hadn't trusted him with the truth about why she didn't want to talk to him. And she'd had plenty of chances.

But could she overcome her fear of rejection?

Sundance whinnied and trotted around the pond, the ducks diving for food rearing their heads at the sound. She patted the gelding and pulled on the reins, coaxing him to slow down.

If she had trusted Ty, would things have worked out differently?

Ty's HEART RACED as George drove him to Jessica's house, but she wasn't home, so they flew to the hospital, but she had already gone, so next he tried the stables. If she wasn't here, he had no idea where to look for her.

If he didn't find her soon and talk to her, he would miss his plane.

But he couldn't leave without talking to her one last time. She was nothing like Paula. She might have said she couldn't live on a ranch, but he didn't believe her. He'd seen her at the stables, seen her with all kinds of people. Jessica could get along anywhere with anybody. Mercy Hospital back home could use a good pediatrician. Hell, the Coopers could use one with all their grandchildren.

"There, that's Nellie," Ty shouted.

George quirked a brow. "Nellie?"

Ty grinned. "Yeah, Nellie's her car. Pull over by the barn."

George nodded and steered the car down the graveled drive, stopping in front of the barn.

"Go get her, son," his grandmother said.

Ty grinned. "Thanks, Grandmother. George."

George raised a brow. "We'll wait in the car."

"The stable owner just had a baby, Grandmother," Ty said. "You might want to go inside and visit. I...I might be a while."

His grandmother's eyes lit up. "Goodness, yes." She waved a frail hand at George. "Help me out of here, George."

George rushed to her aid, and Ty took off for the stable.

"Is Jessica Stovall here?" he asked the stablehand.

The old man nodded. "She took Sundance off about an hour ago."

Ty exhaled in relief, then commandeered a horse and rode off after her. He knew where she would be without even thinking about it. Out by the lake where they'd made love.

A few minutes later, he found her. She'd dismounted and sat down on the hill by the lake, her knees drawn up, her head dropped forward against them. He shoved a lock of hair from his forehead, his heart clenching when she lifted her head and he saw the tears in her eyes.

She looked so lost. So utterly alone. He remembered all she'd told him about her mother's illness. Her father leaving her when she was two. Then the loss of her baby.

How was he ever going to convince her that nothing mattered except the fact that they loved each other when he had already told so many lies?

## Chapter Twenty-One

Jessica's heart constricted when she saw Ty ride toward her. His gaze trapped hers and she froze, unable to do anything but watch him dismount, tie the black horse to the tree beside Sundance and walk toward her. Every cell in her body ached to rush toward him, but that paralyzing fear she'd lived with since her divorce immobilized her.

"I thought you'd gone," she whispered, the tension so thick she could hardly hear the water lapping against the banks over the drumming beat of her heart in her ears.

"I had something I had to do first."

Her heart stopped beating for a fraction of a second while she waited.

His boots brushed the blades of grass as he walked toward her. Without hesitating, he folded her hand in between his and urged her to stand.

"Ty, I can't—"

"Shh." He pressed a gentle fingertip to her

lips to silence her, then gently gripped her arms. "I love you, Jessica, and I'm not accepting any excuses this time."

She clamped her teeth over her bottom lip.

"I realize I lied to you and that it may take time for you to forgive me."

Didn't he know she already had?

"But we can get past it." He lowered his voice. "We can get past anything, Jess. I love you that much."

She shook her head and started to turn away, the agony of seeing him again choking her, but he caught her face in his hands.

"I know you lost the baby," he said quietly, "and I know the rest."

Shock stole the air from her lungs.

"I'm sorry, Jess. Sorry for the pain, sorry your first husband didn't understand, that he hurt you, but I'm not him."

"It wasn't his fault—" she began.

"I don't want to talk about him." He cut her off with a dark look. His heart was pounding. "I love you, Jess. Nothing else matters."

Her chin quivered. "How can you honestly say that? You wanted a legacy. Of course it matters."

He thought about her question a long time before he answered. "Okay, I asked you to trust me once, and I lied about my identity. I'm asking you to trust me this time, so I won't lie to you." His voice grew thick. "Yes, it hurts to hear that you can't have children."

She gripped his hands and tried to tear them away from her face.

He shook his head and caught her hands, squeezing them tightly in his and forcing her to look into his eyes. "But it hurts because I know how painful it must be for you. You're the most tender, caring woman I've ever known, and you should have children. You'll make a wonderful mother."

"That's not going to happen, Ty."

"Maybe not the normal way," he said softly. "But there are other ways, Jess. We can adopt."

She couldn't believe what he was saying.

"You may think that now, Ty," she said, her voice breaking, "but you'd change—"

"No." He suddenly released her, reached inside his wallet and flipped open a handful of pictures. "See these guys here—that's Court and Chad, my brothers."

"You told me you have a big family, that you want lots of kids, boys to help on the ranch—"

"Court and Chad are my *adopted* brothers, Jess." His voice rang with conviction. "But I love them. And I love their kids. And those children at the hospital, hell, I love them, too, and they're not my blood." His voice grew fiercer.

"Being a Cooper isn't about blood anyway, Jess. It's about attitude and family and hanging together in the good times and the bad."

A tear drifted down Jessica's cheek, then another. She'd never known a family like his. "Oh, Ty. But you shouldn't have to settle—"

"I wouldn't be settling." Anger flared in his eyes. "And regardless of your jerk of an ex-husband's attitude about life, I don't have to impregnate you like some damn bull to prove I'm a man." He pulled her into his arms, refusing to release her when she resisted. When he had her settled comfortably within the cradle of his thighs, he tucked a strand of hair behind her ear. "Cowboys aren't animals like you may have heard."

Ty smiled. "And just so you know, cowboys don't carve notches on our bedposts or refer to our women as *fillies*." He brushed his lips across her cheek. "I love you, and I'd only be settling if I married someone else. Because *you're* the one I want."

More tears welled in Jessica's eyes, but this time they were tears of joy. "Oh, Ty, I…"

He traced his finger along the curve of her jaw, his eyes pleading. "Say it, Jess."

She closed her eyes and sighed, then opened them and saw the truth in his eyes. There was no longer any reason to doubt, to fear, to hide.

And there were no more lies.

"I love you, Ty."

Ty stroked the soft indentation of her spine. "Then please, please, Jess, put me out of misery and say you'll marry me."

"I love you, Ty." She grinned and slid her fingers to the top button of his shirt and flipped it open. "And yes, I'll marry you."

He brushed a kiss across her lips. He would do anything to keep this woman. "You're sure you won't mind a big family—"

"I've always wanted a big family."

"And you wouldn't mind living on a ranch? And being a rancher's wife? 'Cause we could get a house—"

"I love the land, Ty. It's the only place I feel really at peace." She kissed him tenderly. "Except for when I'm in your arms."

"Then make love to me, Sugar." He nuzzled her neck. "And this time when I'm inside you and you cry out my name, I want to hear you call me Ty."

GRANDMOTHER MONTGOMERY AND George both whooped with joy when Ty and Jessica came riding back and announced their plans.

"Uh, sir—" George tapped his watch "—your plane. We should hurry."

Ty started. "Oh, right." He threw his arm

around George. "I have a favor, man. Do you think we can call in and get a ticket for Jessica? I want to take her to meet the Coopers."

George *tsk*ed but a smile twitched at his mouth.

"I do have to come back and close up my practice," Jessica said, rushing to the car with them.

"Get in," George ordered as Ty helped his grandmother into the front seat. "I'll phone ahead for an e-ticket."

Ty thanked him and climbed in with Jessica, and George took off. Forty-five minutes later, Jessica and Ty ran toward the terminal. They had barely stopped at Jessica's house for her to pack a weekend bag, and she'd phoned to cancel her Friday appointments on the way to the airport.

"Are you sure your family won't mind me coming with you?" Jessica called as they raced through security.

"No, they'll love you."

George had commandeered a wheelchair for Grandmother Montgomery so they could keep up and was running along behind them, pushing her.

A voice over the speaker announced the flight was boarding.

"Ten more gates," Ty yelled.

Jessica raced after him, her shoes clacking. George took the corner on one wheel of the wheelchair and nearly knocked over a nun. Ty's grandmother shrieked, threw out her legs as if to brake and sent one of her shoes flying.

"My shoe!" Grandmother Montgomery shouted.

"We'll get it on the way back," George called, heaving as he jogged faster.

"Ladies and gentlemen, that was our last boarding call."

"They're closing the gate!" Ty shouted.

"Stop!" George yelled.

Grandmother Montgomery leaped out of the wheelchair and flagged down an attendant. "Tell them to hold that flight to Bozeman! My grandson has to get on it."

"Ma'am…"

"Do it," George ordered. "It's an emergency!"

Grandmother Montgomery dropped back into the chair and flicked her hand toward the gate.

Ty heaved a breath. "We're almost there."

Jessica was panting as she ran behind him.

The attendant started to close the gate.

"Wait!" George yelled.

"Hold the plane!" Grandmother Montgomery shouted.

Ty and Jessica shoved their tickets into the attendant's hands.

The flight attendant narrowed irritated eyes and told them to hurry.

Grandmother Montgomery straightened her silk pantsuit and stood, hobbling to say goodbye on one shoe. Somehow, she still looked dignified, Ty thought, affection warm in his chest. George mopped his brow with a handkerchief.

She hugged Jessica first. "I'm so glad you'll be in the family, dear. You take care of my grandson."

"Don't worry." Jessica hugged her in return. "I will."

"And bring him back to see me."

Jessica nodded and stepped aside for Ty to say his goodbye.

"Thank you, Grandmother. I…I'm glad I came and got to know you."

"And I'm proud to have you as a part of the family." She pulled him close and hugged him fiercely. "Now, be good to that girl. And bring my great-grandkids to see me."

George pounded him on the back. "Don't forget my chaps, Mr. Ty."

"I won't." Ty shook his hand. "And I won't forget you, George."

George straightened, that twitch of a smile in place. "Just invite me to the wedding, sir. I've always wanted to travel out West."

Ty nodded. The attendant cleared her throat. "Let's go, folks. We do have a schedule to keep."

Ty and Jessica joined hands and rushed through the door to board.

Seconds later, they slid into their seats. Ty threw his arm around Jessica and hugged her to him. "I can't wait to make you Mrs. Ty Cooper."

Jessica laughed. "That sounds like a macho cowboy thing to say." She tugged at his denim shirt. "Especially for a rancher who wore suits the last few weeks."

"I hated those danged things," Ty admitted. He nuzzled her neck. "But I will wear one for our wedding if you want."

She kissed him tenderly. "I want you just the way you are, Ty. In your cowboy boots and hat."

## *Epilogue*

Ty squeezed Jessica's hand as the plane took off, his heart full of love and hope and the future.

A bittersweet feeling followed.

Was this the way his father had felt when he'd left the Montgomerys and flown to Montana with his mother to become part of the Cooper family? Ty now understood why his grandfather Cooper hadn't cared about making more money. The Coopers already had everything they needed—each other.

His only regret was that the Montgomerys and Coopers hadn't ended their feud. And that Grandfather Montgomery hadn't accepted him or the Coopers as family.

As Atlanta faded behind him, Ty realized he had a lot of things to tell his brother—all the things he'd discovered about Grandfather Montgomery and the way their parents had parted, the reasons Grandfather Montgomery had held on so tightly to the boys' father, the way his grandmother had hugged him and assured him that one day things might be all right. Dex probably had a lot to tell him, too. In fact, now that he thought about it, Dex had sounded a little strange when they'd last spoken on the phone. Ty had been so absorbed in his own problems and worried about his grandfather that he hadn't thought much about it at the time. But now worry sneaked in on him.

Dex had asked a lot of questions about Leanne.

What exactly had happened back at the ranch…?

* * * * *

**YES!** Please send me the *Cowboy at Heart* collection in Larger Print. This collection begins with 3 FREE books and 2 FREE gifts in the first shipment, and more free gifts will follow! My books will arrive in 8 monthly shipments until I have the entire 51-book *Cowboy at Heart* collection. I will receive 2 or 3 FREE books in each shipment and I will pay just $4.99 U.S./ $5.89 CDN. for each of the other four books in each shipment, plus $2.99 for shipping and handling.* If I decide to keep the entire collection, I'll have paid for only 32 books because 19 books are FREE! I understand that by accepting the 3 free books and gifts places me under no obligation to buy anything. I can always return a shipment and cancel at any time. My free books and gifts are mine to keep no matter what I decide.

256 HCN 0779   456 HCN 0779

| | | |
|---|---|---|
| Name | (PLEASE PRINT) | |
| Address | | Apt. # |
| City | State/Prov. | Zip/Postal Code |

Signature (if under 18, a parent or guardian must sign)

### Mail to the Harlequin® Reader Service:

**IN U.S.A.:** P.O. Box 1867, Buffalo, NY 14240-1867
**IN CANADA:** P.O. Box 609, Fort Erie, Ontario L2A 5X3

* Terms and prices subject to change without notice. Prices do not include applicable taxes. Sales tax applicable in N.Y. Canadian residents will be charged applicable taxes. This offer is limited to one order per household. All orders subject to approval. Credit or debit balances in a customer's account(s) may be offset by any other outstanding balance owed by or to the customer. Please allow 4 to 6 weeks for delivery. Offer available while quantities last. Offer not available to Quebec residents.

CAHBPA13

# REQUEST YOUR FREE BOOKS!
## 2 FREE WHOLESOME ROMANCE NOVELS IN LARGER PRINT
## PLUS 2
# FREE
## MYSTERY GIFTS

🌿🌿🌿🌿🌿🌿🌿🌿🌿🌿🌿🌿🌿🌿🌿🌿

## HEARTWARMING™

🌾🌾🌾🌾🌾🌾🌾🌾🌾🌾🌾🌾🌾🌾🌾🌾🌾🌾🌾

*Wholesome, tender romances*

---

**YES!** Please send me 2 FREE Harlequin® Heartwarming Larger-Print novels and my 2 FREE mystery gifts (gifts worth about $10). After receiving them, if I don't wish to receive any more books, I can return the shipping statement marked "cancel." If I don't cancel, I will receive 4 brand-new larger-print novels every month and be billed just $4.99 per book in the U.S. or $5.74 per book in Canada. That's a savings of at least 23% off the cover price. It's quite a bargain! Shipping and handling is just 50¢ per book in the U.S. and 75¢ per book in Canada.* I understand that accepting the 2 free books and gifts places me under no obligation to buy anything. I can always return a shipment and cancel at any time. Even if I never buy another book, the two free books and gifts are mine to keep forever.

161/361 IDN F47N

Name _____ (PLEASE PRINT) _____

Address _____ Apt. # _____

City _____ State/Prov. _____ Zip/Postal Code _____

Signature (if under 18, a parent or guardian must sign) _____

### Mail to the Harlequin® Reader Service:
**IN U.S.A.:** P.O. Box 1867, Buffalo, NY 14240-1867
**IN CANADA:** P.O. Box 609, Fort Erie, Ontario L2A 5X3

\* Terms and prices subject to change without notice. Prices do not include applicable taxes. Sales tax applicable in N.Y. Canadian residents will be charged applicable taxes. Offer not valid in Quebec. This offer is limited to one order per household. Not valid for current subscribers to Harlequin Heartwarming larger-print books. All orders subject to credit approval. Credit or debit balances in a customer's account(s) may be offset by any other outstanding balance owed by or to the customer. Please allow 4 to 6 weeks for delivery. Offer available while quantities last.

**Your Privacy**—The Harlequin® Reader Service is committed to protecting your privacy. Our Privacy Policy is available online at www.ReaderService.com or upon request from the Harlequin Reader Service.

We make a portion of our mailing list available to reputable third parties that offer products we believe may interest you. If you prefer that we not exchange your name with third parties, or if you wish to clarify or modify your communication preferences, please visit us at www.ReaderService.com/consumerchoice or write to us at Harlequin Reader Service Preference Service, P.O. Box 9062, Buffalo, NY 14269. Include your complete name and address.

HWDIR13R